ZAC'S BIGGEST HITS! VOLUME 1

BY H.I. LARRY

hardie grant EGMONT

Zac's Biggest Hits! Volume 1
published in 2017 by
Hardie Grant Egmont
Ground Floor, Building 1, 658 Church Street
Richmond, Victoria 3121, Australia
www.hardiegrantegmont.com

A CiP record for this title is available from the National Library of Australia.

Cover & illustrations by Craig Phillips
Illustrations inked by Latifah Cornelius

Printed in Australia by McPherson's Printing Group, Maryborough, Victoria, an accredited ISO AS/NZS 14001 Environmental Management System printer.

3 5 7 9 10 8 6 4

The paper in this book is FSC® certified. FSC® promotes environmentally responsible, socially beneficial and economically viable management of the world's forests.

CONTENTS

POISON ISLAND

If it were up to Zac, the Power family would have stayed right where they were, cruising in a jumbo jet 30,000 feet above the ocean.

Zac sat listening to music on his SpyPad with the sound turned right up, finishing off his chocolate ice-cream. The cabin was dark. Around him, everyone was dozing.

It was as warm and cosy as naptime at kindergarten.

'Zac! Take off those headphones this minute and listen to me.'

His mum's cross face appeared beside him in the darkness. She showed him the time on her watch. 12.06 a.m.

Uh-oh.

'You were supposed to have your gear on three minutes ago,' his mum said, half-whispering and half-yelling. 'We can't afford mistakes at this stage of the mission, Zac.'

Sighing, Zac reached under the seat for his backpack. He'd been having an excellent daydream about playing a guitar solo in front of thousands of fans. But there was no chance he'd be doing that any time soon.

Instead, Zac slipped on his jumpsuit, goggles and parachute.

Zac looked over at his brother, Leon. Leon had already changed and was now busy tucking his favourite book, *The Manual of Advanced Electronic Gadgets (4th Edition)*, safely into his jumpsuit pocket.

Again, Zac wondered how he'd ended up with a big brother as geeky as Leon.

Zac's dad leant over from the seat behind them. 'Nervous, Leon?' his dad asked.

Leon was shaking with fear already.

'What about you, Zac?' his dad asked.

Zac shrugged. As if he was worried! He was 12 years old now, and anyway, he'd done this a million times before.

If anything, Zac was bored. What was the point of death-defying adventures if you had to keep them secret? Zac's mates had no idea he was a spy for the Government Investigation Bureau (or GIB for short). Or that his code name was Agent Rock Star.

As far as they knew, Zac was away on another soppy old family holiday. There was nothing cool about that.

Anger bubbled up in Zac. He was just about to say something to his dad when he noticed an air hostess walking towards him. She had a fake-looking smile on her face. 'Would you like a lolly, *little boy*?' she asked.

Little boy! Zac's fists clenched.

'Come with me,' she went on, 'and I'll show you where they are.'

The air hostess pushed Zac towards the back of the plane and through some curtains. A bowl of lollies sat on the bench. Zac took a red one, but the air hostess slapped it out of his hand.

'No! The green one,' she said, sounding tough now that they were alone.

Zac popped the green lolly into his mouth. The sugar coating melted instantly, leaving behind a small disk on his tongue.

'Your mission,' explained the hostess. 'Guard it carefully.'

Then she stepped on a square of carpet and a trapdoor popped open. 'Into the airlock, Rock Star,' she ordered.

Zac stepped down into the dark space beneath the trapdoor. He straightened his goggles and ran his fingers through his black hair. It flopped back into exactly the same place, the way it always did.

He was ready. The air hostess silently counted down on her fingers.

Zac took a flying leap out the airlock and into the black night. A second later, he was falling at 200 kilometres an hour.

Wind rushed past him. It roared in his ears. It sucked his cheeks back hard against his skull. Zac tugged his ripcord and his parachute opened.

WHOOOOOOF!

His whole body jolted as he slowed to a drift.

Finally, Zac's sneakers slammed into the ground below. He'd found the drop zone. He fell clear of his chute and into a commando roll.

He got up and looked around. Where on earth was he? He didn't know what dangers would be waiting for him, or what kind of people he might meet on this mission.

CHAPTER 2

It was hot, steamy and very, very dark. Zac held his hand up in front of his face. Nothing. He couldn't see even a centimetre in front of him.

The darkness made the croaking of frogs and the angry buzzing of insects seem even louder. It was raining hard, and Zac was soaked already.

I'd better get moving, he thought with a shudder. *Before the leeches and mosquitoes find me!*

He felt in his pocket for his SpyPad. The SpyPad looked like a tablet, but was actually way more advanced than that. It was a mini-computer, mobile satellite phone with voice scrambler, laser and code-breaker all rolled into one.

Zac had the turbo deluxe model, which came with amazing retina display and heaps of cool games. But this was no time for playing.

Zac spat out the disk the air hostess had given him and loaded it into his SpyPad.

A message popped up on the screen:

CLASSIFIED

MISSION RECEIVED 11.59 P.M.

The evil Dr Drastic has invented something called Solution X. This is a cure for every type of disease that has ever existed. Sources tell us that Dr Drastic is making Solution X in a top-secret laboratory somewhere on Poison Island.

YOUR MISSION

- Find the secret lab.
- Secure the formula for Solution X.
- Return it safely to Mission Control before Monday at 12.00 a.m.

~ END ~

Suddenly, Zac heard a noise from behind him.

THUNK!

He turned around.

Then he heard it again.

THUNK! THUNK!

Somewhere to his right, Zac heard footsteps. A hand clapped him across the back.

'Rough landing, son?' his dad asked. 'That was Agent Frost playing the air hostess. Hopeless, didn't you think?'

Nothing about spying was ever easy or comfortable, in Zac's experience. He wished they could just get on with the mission. Then he could get home and practise some more Axe Grinder songs.

His mum's serious voice cut through his thoughts like a knife. 'What are our orders, Zac?'

As Zac passed her the SpyPad, he heard a worried voice. 'Mum? Dad? Zac?'

'Shhh, Leon! Anyone could be listening,' said his mum. Then she read the mission on Zac's SpyPad. 'What time is it?'

'It's already one-twenty,' said his dad. 'That doesn't give us much time. We'll have to split up.'

Zac's mum looked at the compass on her wrist. 'OK, Zac, you and Leon head east to the centre of the island.'

Then she added in a quiet voice just for Zac, 'I'm counting on you to look after Leon.'

Zac rolled his eyes. His mum may as well have put handcuffs on him. Even though he was older, Leon was slow, scared and a generally hopeless spy.

Zac wished, just this once, he could finish a mission all by himself. He'd *really* be a hero then.

'Your mum and I will search the coastline,' his dad continued. 'If you see anything suspicious, message us with your SpyPad.'

As his parents left, his mum whispered in his ear. 'We're heading straight home after the mission. You've got to walk Espy.' Espy, short for Espionage, was the family dog.

With that, his parents were gone.

Zac and Leon were alone.

'Ready, Leon?' asked Zac gruffly.

'Um, Zac ... I'm tangled in my parachute.'

Zac sighed. It was going to be a very long mission.

Zac and Leon might have been walking through the jungle, but it felt like they were swimming in glue.

Zac was hot and tired already, and

they'd only been walking for an hour.

Dripping with sweat, Zac stopped to listen for the crunch of Leon's footsteps. But behind him, everything was silent. *Surely not even Leon could be lost already?*

Zac turned. There was Leon, a few steps back. He was standing with his head to one side, listening to something. His glasses were two round patches of steam.

'Listen, Zac,' he whispered.

'Who is it? Dr Drastic?'

'No,' said Leon. 'Frogs.'

Zac gave Leon his *like-I-care* face.

'Hundreds of them,' Leon continued. 'And by the sounds of it, they're dentrobates!'

Zac grabbed Leon's arm. He almost ripped it from the socket. 'Let's just keep moving, OK?'

'Dentrobates, or Poison Dart Frogs,' said Leon in a huff, 'have the most deadly poison of any known animal in the world. If you just *touch* one, it will paralyse or even kill you.'

'OK, whatever,' said Zac, pretending he wasn't impressed.

They walked on in silence.

A few minutes later, something made Zac stop again. He had the creepy feeling that someone was watching them.

Then Zac heard a noise – it was so quiet he wasn't sure it was real.

WHEEWWWWWWWWW!

There it was again!

WHEEWWWWWWWWW!

It sounded like leaves rustling. He hadn't imagined it.

Next, Zac heard a click and the soft whistling sound of something flying through the air.

'Did you hear that?' he whispered.

Silence.

'Leon?' he said again. 'Are you OK?'

But Leon didn't answer. When Zac turned to look at him, Leon had the weirdest look on his face, like he was sleeping with his eyes open.

Leon wobbled unsteadily on his feet.

He was going to collapse!

Zac saw something sticking out of Leon's back. A dart! That was what he'd heard whistling through the air.

Zac ran back, bracing himself for a **WHOOMP!** as his brother hit the ground.

But suddenly a huge net fell from the trees above. Leon was tangled up like an insect in a spider's web. Pulleys dragged the net up into the treetops again, taking Leon with them.

It was a booby trap! And the men firing the darts must be Dr Drastic's henchmen. Was Leon dead or alive?

Zac couldn't tell. His stomach twisted in knots.

HUH?

He was supposed to look after Leon, but now Dr Drastic had him. He'd failed his parents. Even worse, Zac knew he'd failed GIB.

Now that Leon was captive, Dr Drastic would know that GIB agents were on the island, looking for his secret lab.

Whichever way you looked at it, Zac had blown the entire mission!

Zac had only been standing there, thinking those dreadful thoughts, for a few seconds. But it felt like hours. And it must have given Dr Drastic's henchmen the time they needed to reload their dart guns, because …

A hail of darts shot through the darkness, straight towards Zac.

Zac knew exactly what he had to do. On his first day in spy school, Zac had learned an important lesson:

He'd have to rescue Leon later. Right now, Zac had to run.

Dr Drastic's henchmen were getting close.

'Sending two kids!' sneered one of them. 'GIB must be getting desperate for spies.'

Blood pounded angrily in Zac's head. *Kids! How dare they!*

He'd never moved so fast in all his life.

'Stop him!' yelled a henchman. 'He's getting away!'

The two henchmen raced through the jungle after him.

In the heat and panic, voices seemed to rush at Zac from all directions. Which way was forward? Which was up? Which was down? Was he going in circles?

It didn't matter. He had to get as far away from those voices as he could.

Zac had no idea how far he ran, or for how long. Eventually, he noticed the voices behind him fading until, finally, they were gone. He'd outrun Dr Drastic's henchmen.

Hiding himself carefully behind a tree, Zac stopped at last. He had to decide what to do next.

He felt in the pocket of his cargo pants for his SpyPad. Yes, there it was. Safe and sound. He flicked it on.

He could call his parents, but that would mean telling them he'd lost Leon. He could call GIB, but then he'd have to admit he'd blown his cover.

For one second, Zac imagined his mum's face as he told her Leon had fallen into one of Dr Drastic's booby traps. Then he punched in the secret number for GIB. The phone at Mission Control rang.

'This is GIB. Prepare for security clearance.'

Zac held his SpyPad to his fingertip while it scanned his fingerprint. Then –

'Hello, Zac,' said a voice at Mission Control.

'Oh, hi,' began Zac. 'I – *aahhhhhhhhh!*'

'Zac? Do you read me?' came the voice on the other end of the SpyPad.

But Zac couldn't hear it. He'd tripped on a tree root, stumbled forward and let go of his SpyPad. As if in slow motion, the SpyPad was flying through the air. It hit a pitch of sandy ground, then, mysteriously, began to sink.

Oh no! thought Zac. *Quicksand!*

A spy could never be without a SpyPad. Zac had to get it back! He jumped into the quicksand, and straight away his hands closed around the SpyPad. Yes! It was safe.

Right, thought Zac. *Now to get out of this quicksand. It can't be so hard …*

He tried to lift his left leg out. But the quicksand moved underneath him like liquid. It sucked him down even lower!

He tried his right leg.

SQUELCH!
BLOOP!
SQUOOSH!

No luck! He was sinking fast.

Zac knew the best way to get out of quicksand: stay still and wait for someone to come and pull you out. But no-one except for Dr Drastic's henchmen knew even roughly where he was.

An idea popped into Zac's head. What if he let himself sink all the way through the quicksand, until he reached solid ground at the bottom?

Then he could use his official GIB Tramp-o-Socks to bounce his way out. Tramp-o-Socks were like ordinary sports socks, except each heel was fitted with an extra-springy miniature trampoline.

Zac took a deep breath and duck-dived

under the quicksand. It swallowed him up with a ... **GLUB** ... **GLUB** ... **GLUB!**

Zac wiggled off one sneaker, then the other. Even the slightest effort made him feel dizzy. He was running out of air!

But just when Zac thought he couldn't hold his breath for a second longer, he hit solid ground. With all his might, he hurled his heels in their Tramp-o-Socks against the bottom.

Zac shot up, up, up through the quicksand and burst out the top. He soared though the air, gasping for air as he flew.

THUD!

He landed heavily on solid rock. He was right near the mouth of a cave.

Zac crawled into the gloomy cave. Rocks cut his knees, but he didn't care. He was just too tired to stand up.

The cave smelt awful, like dead bat and sweaty armpit mixed together. Zac hardly noticed. A dark cave was the perfect place to hide for a while. Right now, that was all that mattered.

Feeling along the rocky cave walls, Zac came to a ledge sticking out. Relieved, he crawled underneath and took out his SpyPad. The message light was blinking. Maybe someone at GIB knew he was in trouble and was sending back-up!

The message was from Agent Bum Smack (his mum). It said:

Thieves have raided the Government Mint. Millions of dollars stolen. Agent Tool Belt (Dad) and I have been sent to investigate. We're sure you and Leon can handle Dr Drastic yourselves. x

Water dripped on Zac's head. He shivered. Everything now depended on him. Just a couple of hours ago, Zac had been wishing he could finish a mission all by himself. Now that it was really happening, Zac wasn't sure he liked it after all.

Zac switched his SpyPad to message mode. He needed to send GIB a full update. He was typing away when he heard a sound.

It sounded like footsteps!

Zac crouched down lower under the rock ledge. Yes, it was definitely footsteps, and they were coming his way.

He stayed statue-still. He hardly dared to breathe!

'How long's this gonna take, Bruce?' said a man's voice.

Zac listened closely. The voice was the same one he'd heard back in the jungle when Leon was captured. It seemed to come from further inside the cave.

'As long as Dr Drastic says, Bradley,' said the second henchman.

What now? thought Zac.

He could make a break for it and run out of the cave. But he didn't like his chances of outrunning the henchmen twice in one day. Better to stay hidden. He might even learn something.

As though he'd read Zac's mind, Bradley piped up with a question.

'Anyway, what's Dr Drastic got in that lab that's so important?' he said.

'You fool! It's the boss's biggest ever project – Solution X,' said Bruce.

'Oh, yeah? And how's he make that?'

In his rocky hiding place, Zac went red with excitement. This knucklehead was about to give him just the clue he needed to get the mission back on track!

'Seen those poison frogs everywhere? Well, the boss discovered if you boil their poison and add a few secret ingredients, you get Solution X.'

'Wow,' said Bradley.

Zac could tell that he didn't understand anything Bruce had said.

'It's gonna make the boss rich,' said Bruce.

'So where do those little brats from GIB fit in?'

Brats! Zac wished he could shout back something really rude.

'Dr Drastic told the world's governments he'll sell them Solution X if they pay one million dollars each within 24 hours. Guess they don't want to pay. GIB must've sent the kids to find the formula before time runs out and Dr Drastic destroys it,' sniffed Bruce.

Bradley sniggered. 'Do they know he's gonna kill that nerdy Leon kid too?' he asked.

Kill Leon? Zac shivered.

'Dunno, Bradley. All we have to worry

about is keeping Solution X and the kid safely locked in the lab until the deadline passes,' said Bruce.

'I'm sitting down then,' said Bradley. 'Bet we'll be guarding the lab entrance for a while. And I'm starving!'

The lab must be somewhere on the other side of Bruce and Bradley! Zac had to get past them, fast. But how?

Suddenly, Zac had an idea. It was risky, but things were really desperate now.

He turned his SpyPad Voice Scrambler on. He took a deep breath and shouted into the microphone.

'HOT PIES! GET YOUR ICE-COLD DRINKS! ICE-CREAM!'

VOICE
SCRAMBLER
ON

The voice that came out didn't sound like Zac's voice at all. It sounded exactly like a grown man selling snacks at a footy ground.

'Awwwright!' said Bradley greedily. 'I could really go a pie right now.'

'Me too!' said Bruce. 'Didn't know there were snack vans on the island though,' he added thoughtfully.

'Me neither. First time for everything, I guess!' Bradley said.

'HOT CHIPS!' called Zac through the Voice Scrambler.

Bruce and Bradley stood up quickly. They practically fell over each other to be first out of the cave.

'I'm getting a pie and chips. Or maybe two pies!' said Bruce, running.

'Reckon they'll have tomato sauce out here?' said Bradley, his voice fading into the distance.

Zac had done it! The cave was empty. Next stop – Dr Drastic's secret lab.

By now, Zac's eyes were used to the darkness inside the cave. He saw stalactites hanging down from the roof like daggers. Directly in front of him was a long, narrow tunnel leading further into the cave. That had to be the way to the lab!

He set off along the passage. He ran, but carefully. There was a stream running along the floor of the tunnel and the rocks were slippery. He couldn't afford to fall and crack his head. Solution X and Leon would be lost for sure.

Then again, Zac didn't know how long Bruce and Bradley would wander through the jungle looking for a snack van that didn't exist. Yes, they were thick. But *how* thick?

The deeper into the cave Zac went, the narrower the tunnel became. Soon he was on all fours, only just squeezing through.

It got darker.

And colder.

And scarier.

If something happened to Zac down

here, he knew he would never be found.

Just as soon as he thought this, the rocky passage walls started to shake! Deep rumbling sounds came at him from every direction.

Rocks pelted down all around him. The passage was caving in! It was another one of Dr Drastic's booby traps. Zac must have accidentally triggered a trip wire.

Zac tried to speed-crawl forward along the tunnel. But a huge pile of rocks blocked his way. He crawled backwards along the tunnel, only to find an even bigger pile of rocks there. Zac was trapped.

He felt around in his pockets.

He needed something – anything! – to dig with. But Zac had nothing but his SpyPad and a roll of grape Bubble Tape with hair stuck to it.

Wait – his SpyPad! Which had *music* on it. His dad was always telling him his music was up so loud it made the walls shake.

Maybe I could force the rocks out of the way by triggering another rockslide using sound waves, thought Zac.

His SpyPad *did* have awesome built-in speakers. They were unbelievably powerful for something so small.

There was always the risk that even

more rocks would fall, but it was his only chance.

Zac checked the music on his SpyPad.

To trigger a rockslide, he'd need something really, really loud! He found Axe Grinder's latest single, 'Torture Your Ears'.

Perfect! Zac set the volume to ten and hit play.

yelled Ricky Blazes, the lead singer of Axe Grinder.

Axe Grinder
'Torture Your Ears'
VOLUME:
KABOOM!

The force of the sound waves blew Zac across the tunnel. There was no other word for it than *awesome*.

But best of all, the rocks blocking Zac's way forward had been blown apart! Now they were just a big pile of dust.

Zac got back down on all fours. He crawled deeper into the tunnel. Axe Grinder's rock concert had been very cool, but there was no time to waste.

He glanced at his SpyPad before he put it in his pocket. It was already 2.43 p.m.

He must be getting close to Dr Drastic's lab by now. And sure enough, the tunnel started to widen. The stream on the floor of the tunnel deepened. Soon Zac was standing knee-deep in water.

He rounded a final bend. The tunnel ended in an enormous, rocky chamber. Zac found himself on the edge of a lake that took up most of the area.

He took a look around. *If this is the end of the tunnel*, he thought, *then the entrance to the secret lab must be somewhere in this rocky room*. But where? All Zac could see were smooth, hard walls. No secret passages. No doors with codes to crack.

Absolutely nothing.

Then, in the darkness, Zac almost tripped over something stuck into the shore of the lake. He got down low to have a good look.

It was a sign that said 'No Fishing'. There was also a picture of a fisherman looking alarmed as a fish with huge and bloody fangs chewed his arm right off.

It was a piranha!

Zac had seen a dead one once, on a mission in the Amazon. A piranha could chew all your skin off in ten minutes flat. But what would a fish that only lives in the Amazon be doing on Poison Island?

Unless . . .

Suddenly, Zac was certain.

The lab entrance must be right at the bottom of the lake, protected by Dr Drastic's final booby trap!

A piranha-infested lake!

CHAPTER 6

In his mind, Zac made a list of things he'd need to dive into the piranha-infested lake.

First, a diving mask.

But he didn't have one.

Second, an oxygen tank. No, he didn't have one of those, either. GIB didn't think he'd need one in the middle of a jungle.

Third, a piranha-proof suit.

No, he'd left that at home, too.

OK, Zac, he thought. *You'll just have to dive in anyway.*

He took a confident step towards the water. He stopped. *Or maybe there's another entrance to the lab somewhere else?*

But deep down, Zac knew there wasn't. He took a huge breath and jumped in.

Zac swam downwards, careful not to kick too much or wave his arms around. A big splash, he knew, would only attract the piranhas. At the moment, the lake seemed still. Not a single piranha anywhere.

Although ... *aahhhh!*

What was that creepy, slimy thing that

just brushed past him?

In a panic, Zac kicked his legs. He thrashed his arms around. He screamed inside his head, *GET THAT PIRANHA AWAY FROM ME!*

He looked left. He looked right. But all there was floating near him was a gloopy clump of seaweed.

So that's what brushed against me, thought Zac with relief. *As long as I don't make any big splashes, I'm safe.*

But even as Zac was thinking this, he realised he was still splashing around like crazy. The piranhas would find him any second! He had to swim to the bottom as fast as he could.

Down he swam at double-speed.

Near the bottom, Zac saw what looked like a round door with a handle in the middle. The entrance!

Zac grabbed hold of the handle and pulled as hard as he could.

Yes! The door was heavy, but at least it was shifting. He pulled on the handle again. It was definitely coming loose! Only one more big heave and Zac would be in the lab.

Staring hard at the door, he collected every ounce of strength he had. He was just about to heave one last time when ...

A piranha! It was right behind Zac, its mouth gaping open.

It examined Zac's forearm.

Mmm, lunch! it seemed to be thinking.

Desperately, Zac felt about for something to distract it. And there it was, in the pocket of his cargo pants. The entire roll of Bubble Tape with hair stuck to it! Zac broke open the pack and made a giant ball of bubble gum.

The piranha opened its terrible mouth. Its razor-sharp teeth flashed. In a second, Zac had stuffed the ball of gum into the surprised piranha's mouth.

A moment later, Zac was through the round door, through an airlock and into Dr Drastic's mysterious laboratory.

SNAP! SNAP!
SNAP!
SNAP!
TUG! TUG!
CHEW!
CHOMP!
HACK!
COUGH!

What Zac found on the other side of the door was just what he expected an evil science lab to look like.

Every surface gleamed white and silver. Coloured potions in glass containers bubbled and smoked over flames. Across one wall were rows and rows of tanks, all full of frogs. Each frog had a tube attached to it. Zac saw the deadly poison slowly drip-drip-dripping up each tube and into a huge vat on the floor. The only thing missing were the scientists. The lab was completely deserted.

Zac had to work fast. He'd found one of the ingredients in Solution X – the frog poison. That was obvious. *But what are the other special ingredients mixed with the poison to create the miracle cure?*

He had to complete the formula.

Nearby, Zac saw a shelf full of books.

Zac wasn't normally that into books. But today he was. A book was just the place a complicated formula might be written down.

Zac raced over to the shelves.

He grabbed a book. *Family Recipes*, the cover said in curly gold writing. That looked promising. But on the first page, there was nothing but a whole lot of old-fashioned handwriting with the heading, *Mrs Drastic's World-Famous Meatloaf*.

Zac was getting impatient. He had no time for Mrs Drastic's cookbooks.

Faster and faster he searched, scanning every single book on the shelves. *101 Birthday Cakes for Evil Boys*. No good.

Tripe, Liver & Onions – A Treasury of Horrible Treats. Yuck! No way!

Finally, Zac came to a book that was smaller than the rest. It had no title at all.

Perhaps …

He opened it. This book had three formulas inside, but just like the cover, none of them had a title. Each of them listed 'Frog Poison' as the first ingredient.

Suspicious, Zac thought. *Any of these recipes could be Solution X!*

Zac checked his watch. It was 6.36 p.m!

He needed to know which was the right recipe, and fast. There was only one way to find out: mix up each recipe then try them all himself.

Zac rushed over to a nearby cupboard. Sure enough, it was filled with hundreds of glass bottles, each with a weird-sounding name on the label. He grabbed a crusty mixing bowl from a sink and rinsed it out.

As quickly as he could, he threw all the ingredients from the first recipe into the bowl, mixed them together and swallowed them down.

He felt nothing. But then he saw his reflection in the bottom of a dirty saucepan. His eyes were changing colour! One minute they were pink, the next they were gold and the next they were fluoro orange.

This couldn't be the right recipe.

He mixed up the second recipe and swallowed that too. Zac coughed. His cough sounded like a canary singing! Also not the right recipe.

Desperately, Zac mixed together the third recipe. He gulped it down and waited. Nothing happened.

He checked his eyes in the saucepan. They were brown, as normal. He coughed. That sounded like a normal cough too.

This must be it! thought Zac.

He'd found the formula for Solution X! Suddenly, a very loud grinding sound filled the lab.

Zac spun round. The entire bookshelf was turning around – it was a revolving door. Behind the bookshelf, Zac saw a dusty tea-break room, where lab assistants sat reading magazines and drinking coffee.

And there, in the doorway, stood a

pale-skinned man with cold blue eyes and an explosion of white hair on his head. He was wearing a lab coat. Zac saw a name-tag pinned to the chest. It read:

DR VICTOR DRASTIC

Dr Drastic stuck out his hand. 'Agent Rock Star?' he asked.

Zac's mouth dropped open in horror.

But his tongue wasn't acting like it normally did. It unrolled and unrolled and unrolled, and at the end, a whistle blew.

The third recipe had turned Zac's tongue into a party whistle!

Zac was about to be captured. And he didn't have the formula for Solution X after all!

GLUG!
GLUG!
GLUG!
FFSSSSHHHH
!
FWEEEEEE!
BWA!
HA!
HA!

'Step this way, Rock Star,' said Dr Drastic. 'Watch your head on the revolving bookcase.' He was calm and polite, but icy. It was exactly how Zac's teachers sounded when someone tried the 'dog ate my homework' line on them.

Zac felt Dr Drastic's hands on his shoulders. His bony fingers and sharp fingernails dug in hard, like claws. Zac knew there was no running away from a grip like that.

'I knew you'd come sooner or later to save your brother,' said Dr Drastic. 'Couldn't resist trying to make yourself a hero, could you, Rock Star?'

Dr Drastic's cold, blue eyes locked with Zac's. There was something funny about the left one. Zac couldn't tell exactly what it was.

All of a sudden, Dr Drastic reached up and popped out his left eyeball altogether.

He laid it in his palm and showed it to Zac. 'It's glass. I lost my real eye a long time ago.'

Zac had never seen anything as gross as Dr Drastic's glass eye. Unless it was the empty socket where Dr Drastic's real eye used to be.

'Hasn't your mother ever told you it's rude to stare?' snapped Dr Drastic. 'Probably not. She's always too busy spying for GIB.'

He popped his glass eye back in and Zac sighed with relief.

'I bet you hate being a spy,' said Dr Drastic, suddenly cunning. 'You'd much rather make yourself popular with your friends. Being a spy doesn't make you look cool because you can't tell anyone about it, can you?'

Zac nodded dumbly. How did Dr Drastic know all this stuff about him? It made him feel weak and stupid all of a sudden.

So that's what they mean by an evil genius, Zac thought.

'Well, would you like to see your brother?' said Dr Drastic. 'Not to rescue him, of course. Just to say hello.'

He sounded friendly again, as though he were asking Zac if he'd like a chocolate milkshake. His personality changed from nasty to friendly and back again every second minute.

It's scarier than him being horrible all the time, Zac thought.

Dr Drastic strode over to a large silver door on the opposite side of the lab. He flung it open, and inside Zac saw Leon.

But Leon wasn't standing, or even sitting with his wrists bound together with rope the way captives often are.

Instead, Leon was frozen inside an enormous block of ice. The expression frozen on Leon's face wasn't one of pain or fear. His forehead was wrinkled and he had a finger pressed to his cheek.

That's exactly how Leon looks when he's studying or concentrating very hard on something, thought Zac.

Dr Drastic slammed the freezer door shut, smirking. 'Don't fret, Rock Star.'

ZZZZT!
BEEP!

He patted Zac's cheek creepily. 'I left an air bubble in the iceblock. Your brother's still alive.'

Relief flooded through Zac. If Leon was still alive, there was always a chance Zac could come up with some last-minute plan and save him, and maybe the formula for Solution X, too.

Zac looked around him. All the windows and doors in the lab looked really secure. Now break-time was over, Dr Drastic's assistants were everywhere.

There was absolutely no way to escape.

Zac's spirits sank again.

'If I don't get my money, I'm going to destroy Solution X, you see,' Dr Drastic was saying. 'And while I'm at it, I thought I'd do away with Agent Tech Head here, too.'

Dr Drastic walked over to a model of the island in the very centre of the lab.

'I'm going to drop them both into this volcano,' Dr Drastic said, pointing to a mountain on the model. A label stuck to the side read: **MOUNT HUMBLE**.

Zac's mind went into overdrive. He knew there was a volcano on Poison Island, but it hadn't erupted for hundreds of years.

'Ah! I see you're confused. Before you ask, Rock Star – yes. You're correct. Mount Humble is an extinct volcano. Or rather, *was* an extinct volcano.'

Dr Drastic picked up a test tube of powder that looked like pepper from a nearby bench.

'I call my latest invention Eruption Powder. It works like pepper on a human nose. I simply sprinkle it into the crater of the extinct volcano, triggering a kind of giant, volcanic sneeze. And when the volcano's good and hot again, I'll drop in the formula for Solution X.'

'Along with Leon,' said Zac grimly.

'Correct!' said Dr Drastic. 'And you too, now that you're here.'

He pulled a watch on a chain from the pocket of his lab coat.

It was 11.02 p.m.

There was less than an hour until the deadline expired!

'There's a car waiting to take us to Mount Humble,' said Dr Drastic, with an evil laugh. 'I'm dying to hear that giant ice-block sizzling in the hot lava, aren't you?'

Dr Drastic's ute bumped along the rough jungle track towards Mount Humble. Zac's hands and feet were tied together with vines. He was squashed between Bruce and Dr Drastic. Bradley was driving.

The giant block of ice, with Leon still frozen inside, was tied down in the back. It was late at night now, but the jungle heat was still fierce.

As sneakily as possible, Zac turned his head to get a better look at the block of ice. It seemed to be melting fast. Was it possible it might melt before they reached Mount Humble?

'Do you fancy a little car game, Rock Star?' asked Dr Drastic, not waiting for an answer. 'I'll start. I spy with my little eye something beginning with ... S.'

'Sweat?' said Zac, looking at Bradley's stinky, sweaty armpits. The more he played along with Dr Drastic's stupid games, the more time he'd have to dream up a rescue strategy. He had to be careful, though. Dr Drastic would be expecting some kind of escape attempt.

'Good try, but no,' said Dr Drastic. 'S is for "small boy trying to figure out how to rescue his brother and save the day".'

Bruce laughed nastily and poked Zac in the ribs. Zac sighed.

'Give up, Rock Star. There's no escape. You won't be saving your brother. You're not getting the formula. It's O-V-E-R,' said Dr Drastic.

'That spells *over*,' Bruce added.

At the worst possible time, Zac had really drawn a blank. He was out of ideas!

'Look! Over there!' cried Dr Drastic. 'It's Mount Humble!' He clapped his hands with delight.

The ute turned off the main track and started climbing steadily up the side of the volcano. Before long, the ute stopped. Dr Drastic got out and ordered Bradley to unload the block of ice with Leon inside.

Zac hopped along awkwardly. Walking wasn't easy with both feet tied together.

Bradley hauled the block of ice over to the very edge of the volcano crater. Bruce was busy sprinkling something into the crater itself. Dr Drastic watched Zac with amused eyes.

'Yes, Rock Star. That's my Eruption Powder Bruce is sprinkling,' said Dr Drastic in his nastiest voice. He dug out his pocket watch and consulted it.

BOUNCE!
BOUNCE!
HA! HA! HA! HA!
HA! HA!
BOUNCE
BOUNCE

‘The volcano will erupt in five minutes, exactly when the deadline runs out.’

Five minutes!

Things were as desperate as they had ever been.

‘And when the volcano erupts, I’ll have Bradley push the iceblock into the lava. Then you’ll follow. But since I created it, I’m going to save the pleasure of destroying Solution X for myself.’

Dr Drastic fumbled in the inside pocket of his lab coat. He pulled out a tiny jar of bright yellow liquid.

‘This is the last sample of Solution X,’ said Dr Drastic. ‘I’m going to destroy this, along with the formula.’

Dr Drastic waved a piece of notepaper in Zac's face. The formula!

'It makes me sad to destroy Solution X. It's my greatest invention. A cure for any disease or sickness ever known.'

Dr Drastic sighed. 'It's just utterly magnificent, wouldn't you say, Zac?'

But Zac wasn't listening. He was thinking about what Dr Drastic had said. A cure for any disease or sickness ever known.

Wasn't evil a kind of sickness? wondered Zac. *Was it possible that Dr Drastic's evilness might be cured by his very own invention?*

Suddenly, Zac heard a gasping sound. It was coming from the volcano crater!

The ground underneath him began to rumble and shake. Scalding hot steam hissed. Red-hot ash flew through the air.

It was the loudest sneeze Zac had ever heard. He knew at once what was happening.

The volcano was erupting!

CHAPTER 10

Everything near Mount Humble was trying to get away as fast as possible. Even the animals were escaping down the mountain any way they could.

But not Dr Drastic. He stood, calm and silent, on the edge of the volcano crater. He was holding his tiny jar of Solution X. If only Zac could get hold of that jar!

If he was going to have any chance of that, first he'd need to break the vines that tied his wrists and ankles together. But there was no way Zac could reach his pocket-knife.

Just then, Zac felt something brush up against his feet. It was a rat, trying to escape the volcano. But unlike all the other animals, this rat wasn't running. It was fat and lazy and its stomach dragged along the ground.

It was just what Zac needed!

He hopped carefully towards the rat.

Go on! Chew off those vines, he willed it.

The rat might have been lazy, but it definitely wasn't stupid. It recognised food when it saw it. It bit into the vines around Zac's ankles, then his wrists. In a few quick chews, Zac was free.

Zac sneaked up behind Dr Drastic, who was still standing on the very edge of the volcano. It would've been the easiest thing in the world to push him in. But Zac realised he couldn't. He still had to get Dr Drastic to tell him the secret formula.

Suddenly, Dr Drastic drew his arm back. He was about to throw his jar of Solution X into the volcano!

Zac sprang forward. He took a **HUGE** jump. He was like a football super-star!

As if in slow motion, Zac snatched the jar as it spun through mid-air. He cracked open the top and poured the whole lot over Dr Drastic!

For a second, Dr Drastic just stood there with yellow goo dripping down his forehead. Then he spoke. His voice was nothing like the icy, terrifying voice he used before. Now he sounded friendly but slightly confused, like a grandpa woken too early from his nap.

Bruce and Bradley rushed over to help.

'What have you done to him, you moron?' asked Bruce, looking at Zac.

'No, Bruce. It's OK. Zac's my friend!' said Dr Drastic.

Bradley looked at Bruce, confused. But Bruce just shrugged. If the boss said Zac was his friend, then Zac was his friend.

'Don't you know you're in terrible danger, Zac? We're standing on top of an erupting volcano!'

Solution X had worked! Zac had cured Dr Drastic's evilness.

'I know,' said Zac. 'But I can't go until you tell me the formula for Solution X.'

'Oh, well. That's easy! To the frog poison, you simply add ...' And he rattled off a very long list of chemicals.

Zac tried his hardest to memorise it.

'And don't forget the most important ingredient, NaCl(aq),' said Dr Drastic. 'Solution X won't work without aqueous sodium chloride – good old sea water!'

A jet of steam whooshed out of the volcano. Zac nodded. He couldn't stand around for one more second memorising formulas. That would have to do.

'How do we escape from here, Dr Drastic?' asked Zac.

'Take a hang-glider. They're just over there. I've got plenty,' said Dr Drastic.

Zac raced over to a row of hang-gliders. Then he remembered Leon. How was he going to rescue his brother when he was still frozen solid in a block of ice? He looked over at Leon.

Leon was waving! On one side, the volcano had melted the iceblock enough to free Leon's arm.

Zac grabbed hold of the hang-glider. He took a big run up. Wind rushed under the wings.

Zac was flying!

WHOOOOOOOSH!

Zac circled over the volcano, then swooped back down. Leon must have understood Zac's plan perfectly. As Zac flew overhead, Leon held his free arm up as high as he could. Zac grabbed his hand. The entire iceblock lifted off the ground.

But almost as soon as they were airborne, the hang-glider began to drop downwards.

Oh no, Zac thought. *The block of ice is too heavy to fly!*

They were falling straight towards the volcano crater! The lower they fell, the hotter it got. They were dropping faster and faster!

Leon's feet were almost in the lava.

But just when Zac thought they would surely frizzle, the hang-glider suddenly rose again. Up and up it climbed, right out of the volcano crater.

Zac looked down. Flying so deep into the volcano had melted the iceblock completely. Leon was free and the hang-glider was light enough to fly again.

On the ground, they could just make out the tiny figure of Dr Drastic escaping Mount Humble in one of his hang-gliders.

He gave Zac a friendly wave goodbye.

Zac and Leon soared away, high above Poison Island. A few minutes later, they touched down on the deck of a large ship. It was GIB's Mission Control, anchored off the coast of Poison Island. Their parents were waiting for them onboard.

'Mission accomplished, boys?' asked his dad proudly.

'Uh-huh,' said Zac, acting cool.

His mum gave him a big sloppy kiss.

'*Mu-um!*' he groaned, wiping it off.

The floating Mission Control was linked via satellite to the mainland HQ.

'Zac, do you have the formula for Solution X?' crackled a voice through the computer screen. It was GIB's Commander-in-Chief on the line.

'I do, Commander,' he said confidently. 'It's –'

Oh no, the formula! What was it again?

Zac racked his brains.

He had it! He rattled off the very long list of chemicals Dr Drastic had added to the frog poison. Then he remembered there was one last, critical ingredient.

What was it?

'Leon?' he whispered.

'Yup?' said Leon, his lips still blue from being inside the iceblock.

'I can't remember the last part of Solution X,' he admitted.

‘That’s OK,’ said Leon. ‘While I was frozen, I studied Dr Drastic as he was making the formula.’

So that explained the look of concentration Zac had noticed on Leon’s frozen face!

‘The last ingredient is $NaCl(aq)$.’

Zac was amazed. He’d never realised how useful a geeky brother could be!

The Commander interrupted them. ‘Good job, Leon,’ he said. ‘And especially well done to you, Zac.’

Zac tried his best to look modest.

‘Of course, everything you’ve told us about what happened on Poison Island must remain top-secret. The quicksand.

The cave-in. The piranhas. Everything.'

Zac slumped. *How boring!*

'But just because you can't boast to your friends about this, doesn't make what you've any done less important,' said the Commander.

Zac thought about it. He guessed that was true. He'd just have to get used to being an ordinary kid for a while, doing his homework and taking Espy for walks. Still, he'd have heaps of time to practise his guitar solos. Then maybe one day he'd have thousands of fans screaming his name.

Now that, thought Zac with a grin, *would be really cool*.

FROZEN FEAR

First rule of surfing? Never, ever *drop in*. If you're about to ride an awesome wave but someone gets in the way and takes the wave instead, it's called *dropping in*.

Zac Power had read all about it in his favourite surf magazine, *Pipelines*.

Things had been dropping in on Zac *way* too much recently. Zac wanted to surf along all day as though life was one big wave. But things kept dropping in and getting in the way – like school, his parents, his brother Leon and most of all, his job as a top-secret spy for the Government Investigation Bureau (or GIB for short).

But not this time, thought Zac. It was the summer holidays and the Power family was driving to their beach house at Point Relaxation. The whole family worked for GIB, but even spies need holidays.

Zac's surfboard was strapped to the roof rack. His electric guitar was in the boot. He was going to play all night. *Loudly*.

Zac switched his SpyPad to games

mode. Should he play *Grudge Match 3* or *Total Chaos* first? It didn't matter. He had heaps of time to play both. He wouldn't be needing his SpyPad for missions!

On missions, Zac used his SpyPad as a computer, mobile satellite telephone, laser and code-breaker – you name it!

Beside him, Leon was playing games on his SpyPad, too. Not the cool games though. He was playing *Rockin' Calculus*.

Leon worked for GIB as well, but as a home-based Technical Support Officer and Official Gadget Expert.

In the driver's seat, Zac's dad made a left turn. 'Low on petrol,' he said. 'Better stop off here.'

They pulled into a petrol station. It was full of cars towing boats and caravans. Everyone seemed to be going to the beach.

Zac's dad whistled when he saw the price of petrol. 'It's those petrol tankers mysteriously sinking,' he said to Zac's mum. 'It's created a shortage, which has driven the price of petrol sky high.'

Zac's mum nodded in agreement. She pulled her purse out of her official GIB handbag – which came with a laser-guided pocket-knife disguised as a lipstick and Total Knock-out Tissues. These special tissues were injected with a chemical that made you fall asleep on the spot when you blew your nose with them.

Zac shrugged. He knew it was bad that petrol was so expensive. But really, what could he do about it?

Zac hopped out to stretch his legs.

Suddenly, there was a sound of thunder overhead. Air swirled around the petrol station, picking up dust and lolly wrappers. It was strange, because the sky was a perfect blue. But the thunder was getting louder.

Zac shivered. It felt like the sun had gone in. Zac didn't know it, but a huge black shadow was creeping over him.

Leon, watching from inside the car, started banging on the windows. 'Zac!' he yelled. 'Get out of the way!'

But it was too late.

THUNK!

Suddenly, something thumped Zac hard on the back.

In the next second, Zac was lifting off the ground! Something was pulling him upwards!

The wind got stronger. The thunder got louder. Zac's hair blew all over the place. Underneath him, people scattered, screaming. He was 20 metres off the ground and still rising fast.

Zac looked up. He was hooked by his belt onto a cable. And the cable was dangling out of a helicopter!

A man appeared at the door of the

WHÏRRR!
WHÏIR!

helicopter. He shouted into a megaphone.

'Zac Power!'

Zac squirmed in mid-air. If this person knew his name, it must be an enemy agent trying to kidnap him. Zac had to get free!

'This is Special Secret Agent Fox, Airborne Division.'

Zac was level with the helicopter door now. Special Secret Agent Fox took hold of Zac and dragged him inside.

Zac puffed and panted on the helicopter floor. Fox read from a memo.

'This is an official message from GIB.'

GIB! thought Zac. *So I'm not being kidnapped by enemy agents. Things might be OK.*

Foxed coughed importantly and read

on. 'We wish to inform you that your summer holidays have been cancelled, starting from now.'

In that case, things are definitely not OK! Zac had been looking forward to summer holidays for ages.

'Got a jumper, Zac?' Fox was saying. 'It'll be cold on this mission.'

'Why? Where is it?' asked Zac crossly.

'The Great Icy Pole. Know anything about it?'

'No,' said Zac, feeling very grumpy.

And he didn't want to, either.

In a matter of minutes, the petrol station and Zac's family were just a speck in the distance. And so were his summer holidays.

'Here,' Fox said, handing him a disk. 'Your mission.'

With a deep sigh, Zac loaded the disk into his SpyPad.

CLASSIFIED

MISSION RECEIVED 2.54 P.M.

Suspicious activity has been recorded in the Great Icy Pole. Our surveillance tells us that lots of extra planes and boats have been coming and going, seemingly with no good reason.

YOUR MISSION

- *Go to the Great Icy Pole.*
- *Investigate suspicious activity.*
- *Report back to GIB Mission Control within 24 hours.*

~ END ~

Zac's shoulders slumped. 'Lots of planes?' he repeated. 'So what? You could be talking about any airport in the world.'

Fox stared at Zac. 'Have you got absolutely no idea what the Great Icy Pole is *like?*' he blurted out.

Zac shrugged.

'It's the most-remote, least-explored place on earth,' Fox said. 'It gets down to minus 40 degrees there in winter. If you so much as go outside without the proper gear on, your eyes will freeze solid in their sockets and your fingers will snap off!'

Now Fox had Zac's attention. Maybe this Great Icy Pole place would be kind of cool after all.

'Two, maybe three, boats per summer go to the Pole,' said Fox. 'They deliver food to the scientists who live at the research station there. But in the last few weeks there's been a couple of planes a day, as well as lots of boats.'

Zac had to admit, it did sound very suspicious. 'So why's GIB sending me?' he asked. 'Can't they check out what's going on using WorldEye?'

WorldEye was GIB's amazing satellite. It was so powerful it could read a newspaper headline from 500 kilometres up. Normally, WorldEye was invaluable for surveillance work.

'The Great Icy Pole is so remote, it's

out of satellite range. There's no coverage down there,' Fox explained.

'Does that mean –' Zac began.

'Yes, I'm afraid so. Your SpyPad won't work down there. You'll be completely uncontactable.'

That meant no relying on his satellite GPS for directions! No ringing Leon for help with technical questions! No updates or clues from Mission Control during the mission!

This was going to be tough.

'Since you'll be out of contact, we need to arrange a pick-up time once your fact-finding mission's complete. A GIB transport team will be back to get you exactly 24 hours from the time I picked you up. That's 2.05 p.m. tomorrow.'

'What if I miss the pick-up?' asked Zac.

'That can't happen,' said Fox sternly. 'For safety reasons, air traffic is only allowed around the Great Icy Pole during summer. It's almost winter. The cut-off date for air traffic is tomorrow.'

'So, if I don't catch the helicopter tomorrow –'

'You'll be frozen in down there for months,' Fox said, butting in. 'You'll have no food and no way to let us know where you are.'

'Right,' said Zac. 'I'd better be ready then, I guess.'

WHIIIIRR!
WHIRR!

Zac stared out the window, thinking about the mission ahead. Then he noticed a cruise ship sailing in the sea below. And closing in fast behind it was another much smaller ship.

Fox looked over Zac's shoulder at the two ships below. 'The big one's a luxury cruise ship,' Fox explained. 'Rich Americans seal-spotting and looking at the icebergs.'

'And the smaller ship?'

'Pirates, probably,' said Fox.

'Pirates!' said Zac, disbelieving.

Pirates wore eye patches and flew the skull and crossbones. Pirates belonged in children's storybooks, not in real life.

'I know it's hard to believe, but there are modern-day pirates in this area,' said Fox. 'They storm aboard tourist ships and steal watches, jewellery and cash. Sometimes tourists get even get killed.'

'There must be something we can do!' said Zac.

'This area's so remote that it's nearly impossible to enforce the law,' Fox said.

Zac stood up.

'What are you doing?' asked Fox, looking alarmed.

'I've just had an idea,' said Zac.

Before Fox could stop him, Zac had pulled on a jumpsuit and strapped on his parachute gear. Lastly, Zac strapped a wakeboard to his feet and tied the tow rope firmly to the helicopter's door handle.

'Zac! What about the mission?' said Fox, getting angry.

Zac checked the time. 6.43 p.m.

What was Fox talking about? He had plenty of time to complete the mission before the team came to pick him up!

'It's not safe!' said Fox, sounding a lot like Zac's mum.

But Zac wasn't listening. Whether it was good or bad for the mission, Zac couldn't just watch pirates terrorise innocent people.

Zac opened the helicopter door. A gust of cold sea air blew in. Zac took a deep breath. And then he jumped.

Freefall! No matter how many times Zac jumped from planes and helicopters, his heart always ended up in his mouth.

A few seconds later, Zac pulled his

ripcord and his chute opened. Phew!

But Zac knew sky-diving was the easy bit. Tackling the gang of pirates would be much tougher!

With a big splash, Zac's wakeboard hit the water. The helicopter hovered high overhead, dragging him along behind it.

Zac signalled to the helicopter to move closer to the pirate ship. Fox understood him and flew the helicopter closer and closer to the ship.

One of Zac's rules for living was:

NEVER GO ANYWHERE WITHOUT MUSIC TO LISTEN TO.

So, even though he was in the middle of the sea, speeding towards a pirate ship, Zac had loaded his SpyPad with music.

He held onto the tow rope with one hand. With the other, he pulled his SpyPad out from his pocket. He scrolled through his music collection.

Yes! There it was. *Maria Vendetta Sings Italian Opera Classics.*

Zac kept some *really* embarrassing tracks on his SpyPad in case they ever came in handy on missions. Like today!

In his other pocket, Zac had Leon's latest and coolest invention – Assault Speakers. Loud enough to pierce the eardrums of anyone they were aimed at, according to Leon.

Even at a normal volume, Maria Vendetta had a piercing voice. Zac thought she sounded like a cat whose tail had been stood on, a million times in a row.

The Assault Speakers come with a pair of soft earplugs to protect the ears of the operator. Zac squashed them into his ears. Then he hit play on his SpyPad.

Zac turned up the volume on the Assault Speakers. He aimed them at the pirate ship.

'AIEEEEEEEE!' sang Maria.

Zac's eyes watered. The Assault Speakers vibrated. Then Zac turned the volume up one more notch!

Maria screeched. The sound was unbearable!

Zac popped up the telescope on his SpyPad. On the deck of the pirate ship, a collection of rough-looking men were fighting over who would be lucky enough to escape below deck first. Every single one of the pirates had his fingers jammed in his ears.

Obviously the pirates felt the same way about Maria Vendetta as Zac did.

Up ahead, the tourist boat was gunning

its engines. It sped away from the pirate ship as fast as it could. The decks were lined with wrinkly men and white-haired women dripping with diamonds. Zac waved up at them. They clapped and cheered. They were saved!

Zac knew he'd done the right thing, jumping from the helicopter and stopping the pirates. But as Fox hauled him up by the tow rope, Zac couldn't help having a good, long think about the mission ahead.

Zac's spying missions had taken him to some far-off places. And he'd certainly conquered some tough enemies. But somehow, the Great Icy Pole felt different.

It was lonely.

It was lawless.

It was dangerous and bitterly cold.

It felt like anything could happen to you out here. And if it did, no-one would ever find you.

Zac was now an experienced solo spy. But for the first time in his spying career, he was going to be alone on this mission.

Really and truly alone.

Zac's pirate-frightening side mission had eaten up a lot of time. It was 9.12 p.m. already!

They were almost at the Great Icy Pole. Fox had to cram Zac's cold weather survival instructions into half the time he'd planned.

'Here's your snowsuit and thermal

underwear. Also your hat, goggles and gloves,' said Fox.

Zac nodded. Pretty standard stuff.

'And this is … well. It's a little bit special,' said Fox, holding up what looked like an oversized doggy pooper-scooper.

'The Great Icy Pole is one of the world's last true wilderness regions,' Fox continued. 'Naturally, there's no plumbing down there. And the ground is frozen solid. So when you do your business, you just …'

Fox snapped the pooper-scooper open and closed. '… Take it with you!' he finished, blushing a violent red.

'I think I'm going to be sick,' said Zac.

This was a long, long way from being cool.

'Look! Here's where we're going to land,' said Fox, glad to have finished the toilet conversation.

The helicopter touched down behind a towering wall of ice. Even in the gathering gloom of night, the glacier shimmered like sugar. Beyond the glacier, a plain of solid ice stretched right out to the horizon.

Wind howled across the ice. A gang of penguins huddled together for warmth, beaks tucked into their chests.

'This is a covert operation, Zac. There's a group of scientists based at the seal research station over there ...'

Fox pointed. Zac could just make out an igloo-shaped building way across the ice.

'We believe they are harmless enough. Still, you mustn't let them know you're here. The idea is to watch for suspicious activity without anyone knowing they're being observed.'

Zac nodded. He jumped down from the helicopter.

'And remember. Meet the pick-up team back here tomorrow or you're a goner,' called Fox, waving a cheerful goodbye.

Then, in a flurry of snow and icy wind, the helicopter was gone.

Zac switched on his torch and looked around. It was the same blank whiteness in every direction. Even an experienced spy like Zac could easily lose himself in a place like this. He took out his compass.

Zac wasn't used to using such old-fashioned equipment. But he had no Spy-Pad with GPS to rely on here.

Zac paced forward slowly. Icy wind blasted him backwards. It was hard going.

For hours, Zac searched for something – anything! – out of the ordinary. But apart from the seal research station, the entire Great Icy Pole seemed deserted.

Zac started feeling annoyed. *Maybe*

GIB was wrong about the so-called suspicious activity going on down here, he thought.

There was absolutely nothing to see except a lone seal flapping slowly along the ice.

A seal! *How cute,* as his mum would say. Zac bent down for a closer look. There was something funny about the seal. Something about its left flipper didn't look quite right.

The seal flopped onto its side. It looked like it was injured! Zac wondered if there was anything he could do. He didn't know much about seals. But he couldn't just leave behind an animal sick and in pain.

The seal seemed to be going from bad

BEEP!
BEEP
BOP!

to worse. Now there was smoke pouring from its ears.

Hmm, thought Zac. *I'm no expert, but that doesn't look normal.*

Zac reached out and touched the seal. Instead of being warm and soft, the seal felt hard and cold as metal. Then Zac realised the seal wasn't real. It was robotic!

How could Zac have missed all the clues before? The robotic seal had a suction cap for a nose and a strange kind of drill attached to its head. It felt like metal because it *was* metal!

By now, the seal had completely stopped working. Zac flipped it onto its back. There was a row of press-studs down the seal's furry tummy. Zac tore them open. Underneath, he found the seal's mechanics.

Where the seal's heart should have been, red and blue wires ran into a homing device. There was even an in-built clock.

4.07 A.M.

Time was slipping away fast!

If Zac could rewire the seal, maybe it would quickly lead him to the suspicious activity he was looking for! A robotic seal seemed like a sure sign that something funny *really was* going on.

Zac unzipped a pocket on the arm of his snowsuit. He'd stashed a miniature tool kit there, just in case. It was almost impossible to use such tiny tools with his thick gloves on.

But he couldn't take his gloves off! Fox said he'd risk frostbite if he did. A frost-bitten hand would turn black and eventually drop off, dead.

That was about the grossest thing Zac could think of. He kept his gloves on as he tinkered away.

There, thought Zac, attaching one last blue wire to a red one. He flicked the seal on. Instantly, it clapped its flippers and meowed like a cat.

Zac switched off the seal.

That can't be right!

Zac fiddled with a few more wires.

How about that?

He turned the seal back on. This time it moved its flippers perfectly. Only trouble was, the seal kept doing big, loud burps.

One last time, Zac fiddled with the wires. He tried the seal again. That was it! The seal was working, all right.

In fact, it was taking off at top speed across the ice!

CHAPTER 5

WHOOSH! WHIRRR!

The robotic seal sped away. Zac raced after it across the ice. But running was impossible! Zac slipped. He slid about. He fell flat on his bum a hundred times over.

Where is the seal heading? Towards the seal research station, it looked like.

Does that mean the researchers are up to no good, after all? wondered Zac.

By this time, he was panting hard. The GIB training manual said that a spy must be in peak physical condition at all times. And Zac was. But still, he was no match for a machine. He was exhausted.

They neared the research station. Outside was a row of gleaming new skidoos. There was no-one around. The first skidoo even had keys dangling from the ignition. Obviously the seal researchers weren't expecting company.

I'll have it back before they know I've taken it, thought Zac. *And just to make sure …*

A storage chest of firewood stood

beside the skidoos. With all his might, Zac dragged the heavy chest in front of the research station door. The researchers would be locked in, at least for a while.

Zac didn't know whether they were good or evil yet. But he wasn't taking any chances.

Zac jumped onto the skidoo.

Twisting back the handlebars, he revved the engine. Then he took off. He sped towards a huge pile of snow and jumped it.

He flew through the air. Awesome!

By now, the seal had left the research station way behind. It seemed to be heading deeper into the icy wilderness. The homing

VRROOOOOMMMMM!

device inside the seal was obviously very powerful. The seal was heading, straight as an arrow, for somewhere in particular.

But where?

Zac accelerated. He practically flew across the ice towards the seal. He was going to find out!

Then Zac saw a shape looming up out of the gloom. Ahead there were some huge, round storage tanks. Beside those were some long sheds.

It must be some kind of top-secret storage facility, thought Zac.

Zac felt sure he was getting closer to cracking the mission. Good thing too. It was already 5.53 a.m. The GIB team would be there to collect him in eight hours.

Zac parked close to one of the storage tanks, where the skidoo would be in shadow. He cut the skidoo's engine. The sun would be up soon, and Zac couldn't be sure who was watching.

With ice crunching loudly under his snow boots, Zac followed the robotic seal on foot. Silently, the seal slithered over to one of the storage tanks.

Zac watched carefully. The storage tank was fitted with a valve, right down at ground level. Using the suction cap on its nose, the robotic seal anchored itself to the tank. Then, a hose popped up from underneath a hatch in the seal's back. The hose connected to the valve perfectly.

Instantly, the air was filled with a very strong smell. It was a smell Zac recognised. *But what is it?* Zac sniffed again.

It's petrol!

Zac raced over to the storage tank. A metal ladder was fixed to the side. Zac climbed up. On the roof of the storage tank, Zac found a glass viewing-window. He flicked on his torch and shined it through the glass.

The tank was brim-full of petrol!

Pieces of the puzzle began to come together in Zac's mind. The petrol shortage his dad had mentioned. Those petrol tankers mysteriously sinking. Suspicious activity at the Great Icy Pole. And, even more dodgy, robotic seals with drills and suction caps!

Zac's sharp spying brain turned the pieces around and around until he had a theory that made sense.

Robotic seals were drilling into petrol tankers out at sea and stealing petrol. That explained the global petrol shortage.

If you have tankers with tiny seal holes drilled in the side, this would explain why the tankers kept sinking.

The suspicious activity at the Great Icy Pole must somehow be linked to the weird petrol storage facility.

But even as Zac thought this through, more questions occurred to him. *Who is stealing the petrol? And, more to the point, why?*

Zac wished he could use his SpyPad. Then he could discuss his suspicions with GIB. Mission Control would have some ideas. But being out of satellite range meant he would just have to figure it out on his own!

Just then, Zac wished even harder that he could call Mission Control for help. Because, hooning towards him at top speed, was a bunch of thugs on skidoos!

CHAPTER 6

His heart pounding, Zac raced to find somewhere to hide. The thugs on skidoos were shouting and waving angrily. They didn't look too happy to discover they weren't alone in the Great Icy Pole.

Were they from the seal research station? They had to be!

The skidoos roared towards Zac.

Closer. Closer!

Luckily, Zac spotted the perfect hiding place. A big wooden crate stamped with the words, **SPARE SEAL FLIPPERS**. Just in the nick of time, Zac ducked down behind it, out of sight.

'Whoever locked us in has to be here somewhere,' an angry voice growled.

'Yeah, it's probably GIB,' a woman replied. 'I hate those GIB goody-goodies.'

Goody-goodies? Maybe Leon, but not me! thought Zac.

'Hey!' said the woman. 'Footsteps!'

Uh-oh.

'I'll just follow them until I find out where ... ah-ha!' said the woman.

A gloved hand grabbed Zac's shoulders with an iron grip.

'Look who we have here. A GIB spy. Agent Rock Star, if I'm not mistaken,' said the woman.

How does she know my name? wondered Zac. *This gang must really know their stuff!*

Zac's eyes slid across to the woman's expensive-looking watch. It was 6.38 a.m.

He didn't have time to get captured right now!

Suddenly, Zac twisted free of the woman's grip. As fast as he could, he ran towards the skidoo he'd hidden in the shadows. He could hear heavy footsteps behind him.

'Leaving so soon?' asked the man, sounding angry. In a second, he'd caught up to Zac.

'You should lie down,' the man said.

Lie down? Why? Zac wondered. Then …

SMASH!

The man punched Zac in the nose!

'You shouldn't run around when you've got a broken nose, Zac,' he added smugly.

Pain. Zac's whole face pulsed with it. Grey spots floated before his eyes.

Zac bent double. His nose was seriously hurting. Blood trickled from his nose and splashed on the snow.

Snow … That was it!

Still bent over and groaning with pain for effect, Zac was sure the thugs didn't know what he was doing.

Standing up, he chucked the snowballs he'd made right in their faces.

SMACK! SMACK!

All right! Direct hits.

Without looking back, Zac ran for the skidoo. But blood was still streaming from his nose. If he didn't stop it, the splashes of red on the snow were going to show the gang exactly which way he'd gone.

Zac fished around in his backpack for a tissue. His mum had given him some.

Zac held the tissue up to his aching nose.

WHOOOOSH!
SPLAT
CRUNCH

Whoa, what a weird feeling, thought Zac.

The sky went blurry. The snow seemed to swim. He was so sleepy all of a sudden.

Too late, Zac realised what he had done. He'd used one of his mum's Total Knock-out Tissues, the ones that put you to sleep as soon as you held them near your nose. They were supposed to be for enemies!

Zac's eyelids were already dropping. *I'm really in trouble ... I've got to ...*

Before he could finish that thought, Zac was fast asleep!

Zac opened his eyes sleepily. He yawned loudly and scratched his head all over.

Just another day with nothing much to do, Zac thought. *Might have a bowl of Chocmallow Puffs for brekky, play a bit of guitar …*

Zac looked around. He didn't seem to be in his bed. *That's strange … And … oh no! Where are my PJs?*

Instead of being safe at home in his bedroom, Zac was in some kind of laboratory. Somehow, he seemed to be hovering in mid-air. And he was wearing a pair of metal underpants over his clothes!

Then Zac remembered what had happened. He'd accidentally knocked himself out with his mum's Total Knock-out Tissues. The evil researchers must have brought him back to the seal research station and locked him up.

He checked his SpyPad for the time. It was already 12.09 p.m.

He'd been out cold so long, there was only two hours left to crack the mission in time to make his lift home.

But, just then, Zac had other problems to solve. Such as, how on earth was he hovering in mid-air? And what was going on with these metal underpants?

Zac looked up. On the ceiling, directly above him, Zac saw a giant magnet. He looked down. Sure enough, underneath him was another giant magnet. Zac wriggled one way then the other. But he couldn't move!

It was strange. There wasn't anything visible holding him in place. And yet Zac couldn't move an inch!

A vague memory floated through Zac's mind. He was sitting at the dinner table at home. Leon was blabbing on and on about magnets. If two magnets were placed on top of each other, Leon had said, a powerful magnetic field would be created in between.

A magnetic field! These stupid metal underpants are keeping me prisoner in a magnetic field, thought Zac.

Then Zac remembered something else. Hadn't Leon also mentioned something about top scientists using giant electromagnets to power their super computers?

That sounded right ...

Zac knew that an electromagnet was a kind of temporary magnet. It was only magnetic when an electrical current was running through it.

I'm in a research station where there are plenty of computers, so it makes sense that this is an electromagnet I'm trapped in, reasoned Zac. *So if I can turn off the power supply, the magnets will de-magnetise and I'll be free!*

But turning off the power supply to a sophisticated electromagnet wasn't going to be easy, not when Zac was trapped in mid-air wearing metal undies!

Desperately, Zac looked around. If only he could spot exactly where the electromagnet was plugged in.

Over in the corner of the room, Zac spotted a power board with seven or eight things plugged into it.

The electromagnet was plugged in

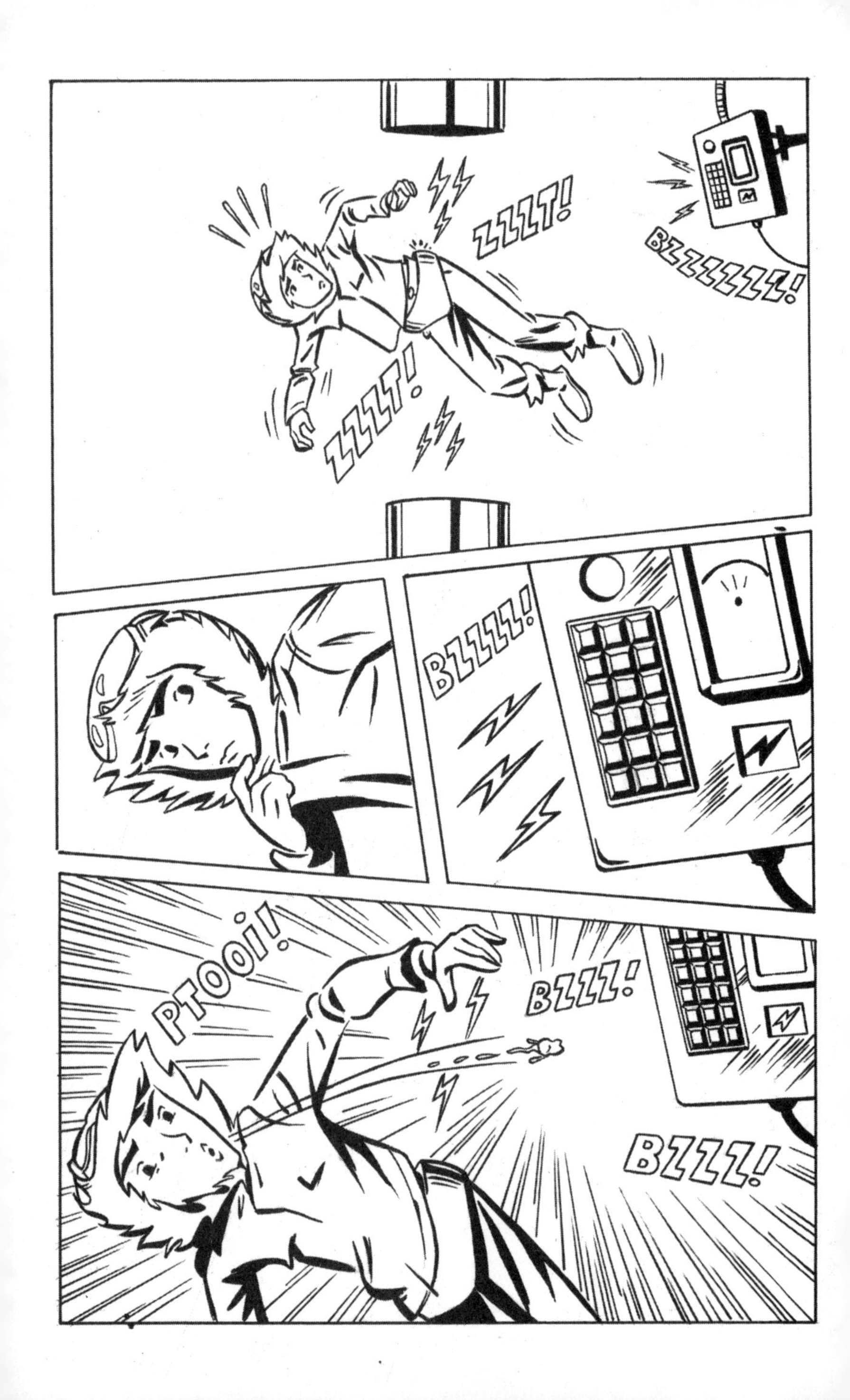
ZZZLT!
BZZZZZZ!
ZZZLT!
BZZZZ!
PTOOI!
BZZZ!
BZZZ!

there too – it had to be!

An idea popped into Zac's head. It was a little gross. But what was that phrase Zac's granny sometimes used?

Zac concentrated hard. He thought of pizza – his favourite Mexicana, with spicy beef, sour cream and corn chips on top.

Immediately, spit jetted into his mouth and pooled in his cheeks.

His plan was working!

Next, Zac thought of chocolate ice-cream sundaes with honeycomb pieces and hot chocolate sauce.

Even *more* spit rushed into his mouth.

I'm ready, thought Zac.

He gathered all his spit into one, huge

mouthful. Then, with all the power he had in his cheeks, he hoicked the world's biggest ever spit-glob in the direction of the power board.

SSSSSPLAT!

With a loud, wet noise, the spit-glob landed on the power board.

FIZZ! SPLUTTER!

There was a shower of blue sparks. The computers stopped humming. The room went dark. Zac had short-circuited the power. And suddenly, he was falling. He hit the ground with a loud clang of metal underpants. But it didn't matter.

He was free!

With the power off, it was pitch black in the research station.

Lucky for me! thought Zac. He still had to work out how to get the metal underpants off. He would have died if anyone had seen him like that!

He could feel a small keyhole in the side of the undies. It didn't take a super-spy to figure out Zac was going to need a key.

Moving fast, he headed for the door. To crack this mission, he still had to find out why the evil researchers were stealing the petrol. And he had to find out quickly!

It was 1.01 a.m. Just over an hour until his flight home.

Zac peered through the glass panel set into the door. Outside, he saw a long corridor. Directly across the hall was a big laboratory packed with fancy equipment.

Could it be the command centre of the entire evil operation?

Scientists and researchers streamed out of the lab. Zac recognised some of them as the thugs on skidoos he'd encountered at the storage facility. But there were plenty of others too. This was no small operation!

'Power must be restored! We're so close now! We can't afford to lose a minute!' one of the researchers was yelling. People scattered all over the building, trying to find out where the short circuit had happened. Pretty soon, the main lab was totally empty.

Clanking awkwardly, Zac made his way into the corridor and into the main lab. And there, on the very first bench, was a small silver key! Zac stuck into the side of the undies and turned it. There was a soft click. Then the undies dropped to the floor with a crash. Relief!

Coolness restored, Zac felt ready to search the lab from top to bottom. Then, overhead, there was a flickering. The lights came back on. That must mean the computers were working again. The researchers would be back any minute!

Zac didn't have much time.

He rushed over to a computer in the very middle of the room. It was labelled 'server'. It looked like the main computer – hopefully the one that would store all the information Zac needed to find out what these people were up to.

Zac tapped a few keys. But all that happened was the computer's screen saver changed from flowers to a photo of a kitten. This was no good! How was he supposed to get into the actual files?

This was where Zac needed Leon's help. But instead he'd have to call on his inner geek and work it out for himself.

Then Zac remembered something. Hadn't that researcher yelled out that they were close now?

Maybe the last document opened on the computer would hold the key.

Grabbing the mouse, Zac went to the File menu and selected Recent Documents. The most recent document on the list was called Operation WorldEye.doc.

WorldEye! thought Zac, surprised. *GIB's*

~MEMO~
TO ALL SKY INDUSTRIES STAFF
OPERATION WORLDEYE - DAILY UPDATE
Petrol storage tanks are at 98.97% storage capacity.
This is almost enough fuel to fire our ballistic missile.
We anticipate total destruction of the WorldEye
satellite system within hours. Great work, team!
P.S. DON'T FORGET, we're collecting money to buy milk
and tea bags for the staffroom. Have you contributed yet?
~

incredibly high-tech satellite system? What would that have to do with the stolen petrol?

Zac opened the document.

He scanned what was written there.

It all seemed horribly clear, except for two things. Who were Sky Industries and why would they want to blow up WorldEye?

The walls of the lab were lined with photographs of important Sky Industries staff shaking hands with dignitaries.

Zac recognised the Prime Minister of Japan, some American senators and … Wasn't that? Yes, it was! The Commander-in-Chief of GIB!

The Commander-in-Chief was standing

with a group of men and women dressed in Sky Industries lab coats. Behind them was a large piece of equipment. Zac could just make out some words painted on the side – WorldEye.

WorldEye! So, Sky Industries manufactured WorldEye? Why on earth would they want to blow it up if they made it?

Unless …

Zac thought about the all-staff email. Sky Industries were collecting money from staff to buy cheap things like milk and tea bags!

If the company couldn't even afford those, the business couldn't be going very well, thought Zac.

Zac knew that WorldEye was the most expensive satellite ever built. Might Sky Industries want to blow it up just so they could get the contract to build a replacement? That way, they'd get their business out of financial trouble. That was it! It had to be.

The petrol storage tanks were almost full. The missile launch couldn't be far away. Zac would have to do something right now to stop it. Otherwise it would be too late!

'Right, then. Back to work.'

Zac's blood ran cold. He recognised that voice! It was the woman with the iron grip who'd discovered him back at the storage facility. And, by the sounds of things, she had all her workmates from the lab with her.

He really didn't want to see that woman

again. She was as tough as nails.

The handle on the lab door turned. In another second, Zac would be sprung.

Apart from the door, there was only one other way out. Without a moment's hesitation, Zac vaulted onto the nearest lab bench. Then, nimble as a monkey, he jumped up and swung from the ceiling fan across to a window high up in the wall.

With less than a millimetre to spare, Zac caught the window ledge. He swung by his fingertips for a second.

The lab door creaked open just as Zac, with a huge effort, hauled himself up and out through the window. Just in time.

THUNK! OWWWWW!

He hit the ice outside heavily.

There was no time to worry about cuts and bruises, though. Zac got up and ran. Just as before, a line of skidoos stood ready and waiting to be used by the researchers.

Or by 12-year-old super spies, he thought.

Jumping on a skidoo, Zac revved the accelerator. It was 1.36 a.m. He had less than half an hour to stop the missile launch and get his helicopter ride home!

Zac roared off in the direction of the storage facility. Wind howled around him. It was snowing hard.

Zac could hardly see two metres in front of him, so it was a minute or two before he noticed.

He was totally surrounded by robotic seals! Waves and waves of seals were moving across the ice towards the storage facility. With so many seals full of stolen petrol, there'd soon be more than enough petrol to launch the missile.

I can stop the missile launch, thought Zac, *if I can stop these seals reaching the storage facility.*

But there were hundreds – maybe even thousands – of robotic seals! How could he possibly stop them all in the next few minutes? Unless …

The robotic seals were full of petrol. Petrol is highly flammable. So …

The plan seemed too good to be true.

Zac could hardly believe he was going to get to do something so cool, and all in the name of saving the world!

Zac dug in his pocket and pulled out his SpyPad. It hadn't been very useful on this mission so far. But now it would be. The SpyPad's powerful in-built laser was going to come in very handy!

Zac aimed the laser at the nearest seal, scooting along behind it on his skidoo.

At first, nothing happened.

But slowly, very slowly, the robotic seal's artificial fur began to smoke.

As he watched, the fake fur caught fire.

Then, flames took over. The robotic seal was swallowed up, and …

ZZZT!
BEEP!
ZZ...ZZZT!
ZAP!
CLICK!
ZAP!
KABOOM!

KERRRRRRRR-BANG!

Enormous fireball!

Smoke! Scorching heat!

The seal exploded, sending a shower of flaming robot parts all over the ice.

BANG! BANG! BANG!

The flaming robot parts set other seals on fire, and they exploded too. Zac had managed to get rid of all the seals and their precious cargo of petrol ... all in one go. It was pretty cool to watch, even if Zac did say so himself.

But Zac didn't have a spare second to stand around and gloat. He had a helicopter flight to catch!

CHAPTER 10

Zac roared off on the skidoo. Where exactly was he supposed to meet the pick-up team again? He thought he remembered.

As Zac scanned the horizon for the meeting point, a terrible thought crept into his mind. Yes, he'd blown up the seals and their petrol supplies. Sure, he'd saved WorldEye *for now*. But what if he hadn't saved it permanently?

Even though Zac had destroyed this lot of petrol, Sky Industries could just start collecting petrol all over again. They still only needed a small amount to bring their storage tanks up to 100% capacity!

Zac thought about Sky Industries and what kind of people worked there. They'd gone to all the trouble of inventing robotic seals just to steal petrol. They'd probably stop at nothing to steal a tiny bit more. After all, they'd be iced in all winter at the Great Icy Pole. That would give them time to get up to all sorts of tricks!

If I truly want to save WorldEye, I've got

to destroy the actual missile, thought Zac grimly.

He checked his SpyPad. It was 1.56 p.m.

His flight home was due to leave in nine minutes! And it was his only chance to get home before all flights to the Great Icy Pole would be shut down for the winter.

If he missed the flight, he'd be stuck in this icy wilderness with a bunch of very angry people from Sky Industries for months and months.

But Zac knew if he didn't destroy the missile before he left the Great Icy Pole, WorldEye would be in serious danger over the months to come.

It was an impossible decision!

There must be something he was missing, some other way to solve the problem.

Zac's mind spun into overdrive. He had an idea. It was risky. But so were his other options. Trusting his spy instincts as always, Zac made a quick decision. He was going to go for it. After all, it wasn't a Zac Power mission without a little risk!

Zac turned the skidoo around. Instead of heading for the meeting point, he went back in the direction of the storage facility. Zac remembered seeing a large silo beside the petrol storage tanks and all the sheds.

That must be where they're keeping the missile! thought Zac.

He sped towards the silo.

He checked the time again. 2.10 p.m. He'd well and truly missed his flight by now.

This plan had better work, said Zac to himself, as a kind of nervous excitement bubbled up in his stomach. It was one of Zac's all-time favourite feelings.

Zac pulled up at the silo. Wasting no time, he marched over to the security door, wheeling his skidoo. It was bolted shut, of course.

Using his patented combination of a credit card, a coat hanger, spit and a ball of string, Zac picked the lock.

Lucky he'd paid so much attention in

that Covert Locksmithing class back in his Spy Training days.

The door sprang open. A giant missile, twice the size of Zac, stood in the very centre of the silo.

Zac rummaged in his backpack for his tool kit. This next part of the plan was going to involve some craftsmanship. Zac had often seen Leon weld bits and pieces together as he was experimenting with new gadgets.

But Leon had never tried welding the driver's seat and controls from a skidoo onto a ballistic missile before!

Zac set to work. Using the laser from his SpyPad, Zac cut the seat part away from the skidoo. Then, with welding gear from his tool kit, he attached the seat and its glass cover to the tip area of the missile.

Zac surprised even himself. In under an hour, the job was finished.

Zac was very pleased. This time, he'd really saved WorldEye – he was going to take the missile with him.

There was only three more things left to do. Find the ignition button, jump into the skidoo driver's seat and hang on tight!

The button glowed green in the darkness. Zac took a deep breath. Then, before he could change his mind about the plan (surely his most way-out yet!), he slammed his hand down on the button.

The countdown had begun!

...10

...9

...8

Zac leapt into the driver's seat.

...7

...6

...5

He yanked down the glass bubble protecting the driver's seat.

...4

...3

...2

...1

He braced himself.

At the very last second, the roof of the silo slid away. Zac shot through the gap in the top and into the icy sky outside.

This was more than flying!

This was **ROCKETING!**

Zac streaked across the sky. At this rate, he'd be back at the Power family beach house in time for the second day of summer holidays.

As he got closer to the beach house, Zac's SpyPad suddenly beeped. It was back in range, and his mum had messaged to say that they were having fish and chips on the beach for dinner.

Hurry up or yours will get cold, said the message.

Cool! thought Zac. His mum didn't need to worry about them getting cold.

He'd be home soon.

Say, about 47 seconds from now!

MIND GAMES

One afternoon, Zac Power was shopping for cool new sneakers at Westbridge Mall.

Zac was a bit of an expert on the subject of being cool. He was 12 years old, and he worked as a spy for the Government Investigation Bureau, or GIB for short.

As he shopped, Zac watched out for people he knew. He didn't want anyone from school to think he cared how he looked. That would be try-hard.

At Hot Diggity, the hot-dog shop, Ann and her best friend Lucy were giggling into their milkshakes. Girls!

His favourite CD shop, Tunez, was full of kids from school. The whole world seemed to be hanging out at Westbridge. But Zac slipped by them all, unnoticed.

Zac headed towards Sports Station. Inside, the music was so loud the walls were shaking. It was rock music, the only kind Zac liked. Sports Station had the best sneakers at Westbridge. Zac's favourites were a pair with green and yellow stripes on the side.

Zac picked them up. Straight away, a sales guy bounced over. A plastic name tag on a cord around his neck read, 'Davo'.

'You all right, mate?' asked Davo.

'Can I try these? Size...uh...eight?' Zac said.

'No worries. I'll go check out the back.'

The sales guy disappeared into the storeroom. Zac waited. He looked at some T-shirts. No sales assistant. He picked up a magazine and checked out the photos of kids in the latest clothes skateboarding down stair-rails. Still no Davo.

What is he doing out there?

Suddenly, Davo reappeared, a shoebox in his hand and a weird look on his face.

'We didn't have size eight in the green and yellow. But why don't you try these on instead?'

He opened the box. Inside, Zac saw a pair of the ugliest sneakers *ever*. They were grey, the colour of belly-button fluff. The soles were twice as thick as ordinary sneakers. They were covered in wires and flashing lights.

'Nah, that's OK, thanks,' said Zac, heading for the door.

'Come on! They're limited edition. I guarantee no-one else'll have a pair like them.'

Zac rolled his eyes. 'No-one would want to!'

Davo pulled the grey sneakers out of the box.

'Just try 'em.'

Heaving a big sigh, Zac grabbed the shoes and pulled them on. They felt even worse than they looked!

As soon as his foot was inside, clamps grabbed Zac's ankles. He stood up and couldn't help wobbling as he took a step. Each sneaker must have weighed about 100 kilos.

'What do you think?' asked Davo.

Zac shook his head. 'I might wait 'til you get the others in.'

'Oh, come on, Zac. Just take them.'

Zac? How did this guy know his name?

Davo leant over to pick up the box. His name tag flipped over and Zac caught a glimpse of the back.

Was it? Yes, it was! The GIB crest!

Davo grabbed Zac by the arm and whispered in his ear, 'They're yours, OK? Now get out of here.'

Before Zac could stop him, Davo disappeared with Zac's old sneakers. Great! Now Zac had to walk all the way home in the weird grey sneakers.

He stepped out of Sports Station. Ann and Lucy had finished their milkshakes and gone home. Perhaps he was safe...

Then...

KERR-BOOOOOM!

There was an ear-splitting explosion. A cloud of white smoke. The gross grey sneakers had exploded!

Zac shot up off the ground. He flew through the air, propelled by his exploding sneakers. They had the force of ten rockets. No, make that 100 rockets!

Zac shot past Hot Diggity. Tunez was a blur. He was flying towards a set of lifts. The metal doors were closed. Yikes! He was going to smash right into them.

At the very last second, the lift doors opened and suddenly, Zac was falling. He looked up and saw the lift stuck high above him. He was falling straight down the lift well.

SHOES
TRAVEL
PETS
!
FSSSH
BA-BOOM!
WHOOSH!
DING
?
!

Round and round, faster and faster he fell in a mid-air forward roll.

At the bottom of the lift well, Zac landed with a thud on hard, cold concrete. Lucky he had been taught how to land safely during GIB training, or he would have broken a bone for sure.

The lift doors opened with a ping.

Zac was in an underground car park. Parked nearby was a white van with a satellite dish on the top. The door opened and a strong pair of arms dragged Zac into the back.

The door slammed shut and, with a screech of tyres, the van took off.

Zac looked down at his feet. The

exploding sneakers were totally gone. All that was left was a very holey, smoky pair of socks.

'Hello, Zac,' said the strong-armed man, who was driving the van. 'I've been expecting you.'

‘I’m Agent-In-Training Gorman, GIB Transport Division,’ said the man. ‘Hope that wasn’t too uncomfortable, Zac,’ he went on, looking guiltily at Zac’s socks. ‘I’ve just transferred from Stationery and Supplies, actually. You’re my first agent pick-up.’

Zac remembered his first mission.

He smiled at Gorman. It wasn't easy being the new guy.

'Do you know the way to the airport, Zac?' asked Gorman.

'The airport? Why? What's my mission?' said Zac.

Gorman fished around in his pockets. 'It's somewhere in here,' muttered Gorman to himself.

At last he found what he was looking for. He handed Zac a small metal disc.

Zac loaded the disc into his SpyPad. Every GIB spy had a SpyPad. It looked sort of like an electronic game, but really it was a tablet with in-built GPS, laser and code-breaking apps, all rolled into one.

CLASSIFIED

MISSION INITIATED 9 A.M.

Unknown hostiles are hacking into the computer system controlling GIB's satellite system, WorldEye. WorldEye is so powerful it can read a newspaper headline from 500 kilometres up. The software is protected by encrypted passwords and high-level firewalls. Still, the hackers have managed to breach every firewall but one.

YOUR MISSION

- Locate hackers.
- Discover why they want to hack into WorldEye.
- Prevent breaching of final firewall

~ **END** ~

This was bad!

Only one firewall standing between WorldEye and a bunch of criminals!

'What does Leon think?' asked Zac, as the van turned onto the freeway to the airport.

Leon, Zac's brother, was a Technical Support Officer with GIB. If anyone knew how to handle computer hackers, it was Leon.

'Leon's tracked the hackers to the city of Bladesville,' said Gorman.

Zac fought back a proud smile. Sometimes nerdy brothers really did come in handy.

'You wouldn't be smiling if you knew

anything about Bladesville,' said Gorman. His eyes widened. 'I've heard it's one of the meanest, toughest, dirtiest cities in the whole world.'

Zac said nothing. Whatever Bladesville had in store for him, he could deal with it. Couldn't he?

'Oh, yeah,' Gorman went on. 'Leon reckons it'll take the hackers 24 hours to breach the last firewall.'

Only 24 hours? Zac did some quick calculations in his head.

Now he was freaking out!

'Says here the mission started at 9 a.m. today, so that means I've only got until 9 a.m. tomorrow to fly to Bladesville and stop the hackers. And it's – ' Zac glanced at his SpyPad – 'already 6.51p.m.!'

Gordon looked guilty for a moment.

'Yeah, sorry about the delay in getting you on the mission, Zac. First time and everything, you see.'

Gorman coughed nervously. But Zac could see there wasn't any point getting angry. Gorman was doing the best he could. Was it his fault his best was, um, not really very good?

Gorman opened the van's glovebox.

'I nearly forgot these,' he said, passing Zac a pair of wraparound glasses with a slick-looking computer game controller attached.

'These aren't going to explode, are they?' Zac asked, thinking of the sneakers.

'No, they're virtual-reality glasses,' said Gorman vaguely.

Zac put the glasses on.

It looked exactly like he was sitting in the cockpit of a fighter jet. Zac grabbed the controller. Through the glasses, it looked like he was touching real fighter-jet controls.

'Woah!' said Zac. It was the most realistic flight simulator he had ever seen.

'Isn't it incredible?' said Gorman. 'Ever piloted a fighter-jet before?'

Zac hadn't, but he couldn't wait to try. He took hold of the steering yoke. He sped off down the tarmac. He engaged the throttle. Then, with a loud, realistic whoosh of air, he was airborne!

Up Zac flew. He burst through the clouds. He was 20,000 feet and climbing fast.

He fiddled with the controls. One was for speed, one was to turn left and right. *This flying thing isn't so hard,* thought Zac.

Then Zac heard a warning siren.

A message flashed on his virtual computer screen.

...***STORM ALERT!***...

The sky went dark. Purple lightning slashed the sky. The plane shook violently. Zac's fighter had been struck!

The jet jerked one way, then the other. Zac couldn't get control of the steering. His computer screen flashed again.

...*LOSING ALTITUDE!*...

The plane nose-dived.

Helpless, Zac watched the altitude drop from 20,000 to 10,000 feet in a few seconds. He broke through the clouds. Right below was a mountain range. He was going to crash!

Zac winced and braced himself for impact. The fighter spun onto its back and slammed into the mountains. It burst into flames.

...*GAME OVER! YOU LOSE!*...

Zac ripped off the virtual-reality glasses.

FWOOOOSH!
WARNING! WARNING!
BEEP! BEEP!
GAME OVER

He was sweating. The plane crash had felt so real!

'All right, Zac?' asked Gorman.

Zac nodded.

'Computer games are so advanced these days,' Gorman continued. 'And so addictive! They really play mind games with you.'

Ghost-white, Zac nodded.

'Well, don't worry. We're at the airport now,' said Gorman cheerfully.

The van turned into a secret side entrance. The tarmac was just ahead. And there, waiting for Zac, was a miniature fighter jet.

'Probably should've told you before,'

said Gorman, absent-mindedly. 'You're flying yourself to Bladesville. The flight simulator was your training.'

Zac said nothing.

A spy always keeps his cool.

'That's OK with you, isn't it, Zac?'

Zac strode casually across the tarmac towards the mini-fighter jet. He raced up the stairs to the cockpit. The controls looked almost the same as the ones in the flight simulator. A radio headset sat on the pilot's seat.

Zac put it on and heard a voice.

'Zac Power, this is Air Traffic Control.

The time is 8.09 p.m. Weather conditions fine. You're cleared for take-off on runway three.'

Zac took hold of the yoke. He engaged the throttle and the engine growled.

The fighter jet taxied across the tarmac. Zac angled the yoke upwards and pushed harder on the throttle. The jet gathered speed. Then, with a loud thump as the wheels folded up, Zac was in the air.

But this time, it was for real!

Steadily, Zac climbed. He pierced the clouds. The sun was out and there was no wind. Perfect flying conditions!

Zac tipped the yoke forward. The plane dipped down. He pulled the yoke up again.

The plane shot upwards. He pulled the yoke sharp right. The jet flipped over onto its side!

Cool! Zac tried the left-hand side. He shot into a wicked loop-the-loop.

Maybe this wasn't getting him to Bladesville as fast as possible. But it was *so* worth it!

A voice crackled in Zac's radio headset.

'Come in, Zac Power.'

'Power here,' said Zac, as confidently as he could.

'Weather conditions in your airspace have declined,' said Air Traffic Control. 'A freak electrical storm's heading your way.'

Zac looked around. The brilliant sun-

shine had gone. Heavy black clouds were everywhere.

The fighter started to rattle and bump. Turbulence!

'Suggest emergency landing,' said Air Traffic Control.

Zac looked at the time.

10.48 P.M.

If Zac landed now, it'd take him forever to get to Bladesville and find those hackers. Freak storm or not, Zac was going to have to keep flying.

'Request permission to continue to Bladesville,' said Zac.

There was silence from Air Traffic Control. The fighter roared into a really rough air pocket. The entire cockpit shook. For a second, radio communication dropped out.

The radio came back on. 'Permission granted. Proceed at your own risk.'

Grimly, Zac flew on. Wind rattled the windscreen. The plane lifted and dropped in the wind.

It was worse than a fun-park ride.

The fighter was equipped with rocket-assisted ejector seats. Zac checked where the lever was, just in case.

Beside the lever, Zac noticed a button labelled 'Vertical Supersonic'.

Zac took a deep breath. Could this button possibly do what he hoped? If it climbed at supersonic speed, there was a chance Zac could make it above the storm and out of danger.

Just then, the cockpit lit up as lightning crackled across the sky. These were the conditions that made Zac crash the simulator!

Without thinking, Zac slammed his hand down on the Vertical Supersonic button. Immediately, the fighter jet responded. The nose rose steeply until the plane was speeding straight up.

Then...

BOOOOOOOOOOOM!

A sonic boom!

Zac had broken the speed of sound. He'd gone supersonic!

SLAM!
BOOM
WHOOOSH!
RRUMBLE!

He streaked upwards, leaving the storm behind him. His hands shook. Going Vertical Supersonic had been as scary as it was awesome.

Zac jammed on the brakes. He'd been flying so fast he'd hardly noticed he was almost in Bladesville.

Now he had to figure out how and where to land. He had a closer look at the instruments and dials flashing on the dashboard. He noticed a button labelled 'Engage Stealth Shield'.

Zac hit the button.

Instantly, his mini-fighter jet vanished from his radar screen. The stealth shield had turned him invisible!

Zac looked up the location of Bladesville Airport. It was 50 kilometres out of town. He checked the time.

It was already 11.34 p.m.!

Then Zac had an idea.

If his mini fighter jet was invisible, he could land wherever he wanted!

With that decided, Zac flew downwards. Skyscrapers stuck up everywhere. The streets were choked with cars and people.

The tallest skyscraper had a huge logo

on the side. MindLab. They were some kind of games company. The top of the MindLab building was going to make the perfect landing strip for an invisible mini-fighter jet.

Coming in to land, Zac couldn't help switching on the PA system, even though he was alone. This piloting stuff was pretty fun.

'Ladies and gentlemen, this is Captain Zac Power speaking.'

His landing was perfect. Not a single bump. Maybe, in another life, Zac could have been a pilot. But he had to shut those thoughts out. He was a spy. He always would be. Zac allowed himself the smallest of sighs.

Zac popped open the invisible cockpit door. He stuck his head out and looked around the top of the MindLab building. A beefy security guard was standing near the staircase from the roof into the building.

As usual, Zac had his abseiling gear in his backpack. He'd get down the quick way. Over the side of the building. All 200 storeys!

Around floor 103, Zac's SpyPad beeped. He fished about in his pocket awkwardly – abseiling a hundred floors above a busy street wasn't the perfect time to be checking messages.

It was a cryptic message from GIB Mission Control.

ZIIP!
BEEP! BEEP!
DING DING
BEEP BEEP
HONK
CAFE
FOOD

Go to Electric Eel Workshop

Shop 13, Dank Alley, Bladesville.

Your contact is Mrs X.

Zac made it down to the street and looked around. He'd never seen such a strange place. It was the middle of the night, but it was still burning hot. Stalls selling food and fake electronic games were everywhere. Music blasted. A monorail snaked overhead.

According to his SpyPad's GPS, Dank Alley was not far.

He zigzagged down alleys smelling of fish and rubbish. Finally, he found Dank Alley. Shop 13 was down the end, nearly hidden by steam rising up from a gutter.

A sign on the grimy door read, 'We're closed, so go away'.

Zac knocked anyway. 'Mrs X?' he called. 'It's Zac Power.'

Six or seven deadlocks opened. The door swung open a crack. In the dim light, Zac saw a woman about his own height. Her face was wrinkled, her hair white. A tattoo of an eel twisted up her arm. She looked 120 years old!

'Come,' she said in a funny accent. With a crooked old finger, she directed Zac to the back of the shop. There stood something covered with a dusty old sheet. Whatever it was, Zac couldn't imagine needing it for his mission.

Mrs X pulled off the sheet. Underneath, was a brand-new motor scooter. There were millions just like it roaring down the streets of Bladesville. Only those ones were dented and rusty. This one gleamed silver.

'One important addition,' said Mrs X. She pointed at a lever on the front. 'Pull up, you fly. Pull down, you sing karaoke.'

'This is a karaoke hover scooter?' said Zac, disbelieving. Mrs X nodded.

'You go. Tell GIB I send big bill, very soon.' Mrs X started to cackle to herself.

Zac was wheeling the scooter out into Dank Alley when his SpyPad beeped.

'You have one new voice message,' the screen flashed.

Zac put the SpyPad to his ear.

'Hello, Zac. Welcome to Bladesville,' said a voice – it sounded like a teenager.

Could this be one of the hackers? wondered Zac. The voice sounded so young. Then again, Zac and Leon were way better with technical stuff than their mum and dad. Zac's dad couldn't even work the DVD player!

The message went on. 'We've been tracking you since you took off. Wonderful thing, WorldEye. Anyway, we found your invisible fighter jet. Pretty cocky, landing on the MindLab building. If you want to live, you better get out of here. Right now.'

The hackers were onto him! And, by the sounds of things, they'd managed to gain partial control of WorldEye even without breaching the final firewall.

Zac's mission suddenly felt a lot more dangerous.

Zac crouched in a dark doorway, hidden in shadow. He clutched his SpyPad tight. He was in a foreign city and totally alone. His hands weren't shaking, exactly. But he'd have to admit that the message from the hackers made him edgy.

He punched in the number for GIB Tech Support.

Leon picked up the phone. A friendly voice! Relief flooded through Zac.

'Listen to this message, Leon. I'll patch it through now,' said Zac.

Leon listened.

'Nasty,' he said. 'But don't worry. I'll trace the message. Could lead you straight to the hackers.'

Zac waited nervously.

Finally, Leon had something. 'The message seems to have come from somewhere within a one-kilometre radius of your current location,' he said.

It was 2.47 a.m. already. Zac had to get a move-on!

'Can't you tell me anything else?' asked

Zac. 'It'll take me weeks to search a square kilometre in this place.'

But Leon couldn't. 'They've got a very effective location-scrambling device, Zac. These hackers are pretty clued in.'

Great! That was all Zac needed to hear!

Zac wasn't sure what to do next, so he replayed the message. This time, he thought he heard something in the background. Music? Yes, it was!

He listened again.

It sounded like 'Rotten Lies' by Nemesis, one of his favourite bands. But the singing was terrible – the voice was nothing like the lead singer's.

Zac toyed with the handlebars of his

new karaoke hover scooter.

Something clicked.

Karaoke! Bladesvillians *loved* karaoke. The hackers must have sent the message from a karaoke bar.

Zac flicked his SpyPad to GPS mode.

Find karaoke bars within one kilometre from here, he typed.

A single name popped up on the screen. The Golden Eardrum Karaoke Cave. Zac jumped on his hover scooter and sped straight there.

It didn't take Zac long to find the Golden Eardrum – it had a bright purple front door and a giant rotating ear on the roof.

CAFE
WHOOSH!
GOLDEN EARDRUM
KARAOKE
KARAOKE
BAKERY
NOODLES
HONK
Z MART
DONUTS
CUISINE
BEEP!
HONK!

He needed to go in and look around without attracting attention. But he knew most of the other customers would be grown-ups. A 12-year-old on his own would really stand out in the crowd.

Then Zac remembered something.

A couple of months ago, Leon had given him a new gadget to road-test on a mission. Zac had stuffed it into his backpack and forgotten all about it.

Zac ducked into a nearby alley and pulled out the Protector Projector. The Protector Projector created incredibly realistic 3D holograms.

All Zac had to do was film himself with the Protector Projector. The Projector would then transmit a hologram of whatever Zac was doing in the footage. It would look absolutely real!

I've got to make it look like I'm doing karaoke, thought Zac. *Then, everyone will be watching my hologram on stage while the real me can look around the Golden Eardrum.*

He looked around the alley carefully. Yes, it seemed deserted. He was going to have to film himself singing here.

Zac set the Protector Projector to Record mode. *They like Nemesis at the Golden Eardrum...better do a Nemesis song,* thought Zac.

'Drivin' down the highway, feelin' pretty cool,' Zac sang.

How embarrassing! Zac couldn't just stand there, either. To make this performance look real, he'd have to dance too. Secretly, he'd always dreamt of being a rock star. Now he had to pretend he really was one!

'No place to go today, not even school,' Zac wailed, getting warmed up.

This chorus bit was actually pretty cool. Zac played a solo on the air guitar. For once, his dream of becoming a rock star and his spying missions were fitting together perfectly!

Zac hit Stop on the Protector Projector and headed for the Golden Eardrum. He was going to track down those hackers if it was the last thing he did. And his hologram was going to put on one awesome show!

A queue snaked out of the Golden Eardrum. Men in suits shouted and swayed. Women in their best dresses teetered in high-heeled shoes.

None of these people look like hackers, thought Zac. *Actually, they look like an ad for staying at home with a good DVD.*

Just then, the bouncer unclipped the

velvet rope blocking the entrance. He waved a couple through, and Zac tagged along behind. He was inside!

The Golden Eardrum was absolutely packed. In a crowd like this, the hackers could be anywhere.

Through a smoky haze, Zac saw a stage at the front of the room. Above that, there was a large screen. Song lyrics appeared on the screen so you could follow along when you were up on stage singing.

Along one wall, he saw what looked like phone booths. They were sound-proof karaoke practice booths.

Up on stage, a trio of girls were finishing a horrible, soppy love song.

Now's my chance! Zac thought to himself. He sneaked up to the stage. He hid the Protector Projector under a nearby table and switched it on. A beam of light shot out. Zac aimed it at the stage.

Leon's gadget worked! For there, up on stage, was an absolutely realistic hologram of Zac singing a Nemesis song at the top of his voice.

The audience whistled and cheered.

Time for the real Zac to get to work!

Zac scanned the crowd. A group of teenagers stood by the stage, watching the hologram of Zac's awesome performance. *Could they be the hackers?* They looked younger than everyone else in the Golden

Eardrum. And it made sense that computer whizzes would be kids.

Just then, Zac's hologram made a strange choking noise.

What? That wasn't in the song!

'Don't wanna be a grown-up, oh no no no,' sang the hologram.

Then came the choking noise again.

'Oh no no no – '

'Oh no no no – '

The hologram was jammed! It repeated the same line over and over, like a CD skipping. Zac's cover was blown!

A second later, Zac turned back to the teenagers. But they were gone!

Then Zac saw them disappearing into

the karaoke practice booth second from the left. He counted seven people going into the booth.

That doesn't seem right, thought Zac. *How could so many kids fit into such a small space?*

Sticking to the shadows, Zac tiptoed over to the booth. He took a deep breath and threw open the door.

The booth was completely empty!

Looking down, Zac noticed a trapdoor cut into the floor.

The handle was still warm!

Zac heaved open the trapdoor. Down in the gloom, Zac saw a ladder. *Probably leads to the hackers' underground lair,* thought Zac.

KARAOKE
?
TIP
TOE
TIP
TOE
TIP
TOE

Zac had no idea if the hackers would still be down there. But there was only one way to find out. As quietly as he could, Zac sneaked down the ladder.

He looked around. With its white walls and bare light bulbs, the room looked like an ordinary storeroom. The only difference was, it was filled with rows of the latest computers.

If this is the hackers' secret lair, thought Zac, *where are the hackers?*

There was absolutely no-one around.

Frustration bubbled up in Zac. He'd been so close! Yet somehow the hackers had slipped away.

Downbeat, Zac took another look

around. The hackers had left no trace behind.

No dropped wallet.

No mobile phone.

Not even a single hair.

Except...

What on earth was *that thing*, sitting on the floor?

CHAPTER 7

It was the weirdest thing Zac had ever seen. It was shaped like a normal game console, but where the left, right, up and down buttons should have been, this thing had wires hanging out. Attached to the end of the wires was a shiny metal helmet. It looked like a high-tech version of Zac's mum's colander!

Zac dug out his SpyPad and snapped a photo. Then he emailed a copy through to Tech Support back at GIB Mission Control. If there was anyone nerdy enough to know what this was, it was Leon.

A few seconds later, Zac's SpyPad rang.

'That's MindLab's latest console, the MindGame 3000!' said Leon, sounding like he was about to pop with excitement.

'What does it do?' asked Zac.

'It's like an ordinary game console, but instead of pressing buttons, you *think* your next move. You can control any computer game just with your mind!'

It sounded cool, but it wasn't going to lead Zac to the hackers.

Leon was still carrying on about the MindGame 3000. 'This is totally amazing! They're not even out on the market yet!' Leon was saying as Zac hung up.

Zac found a door at the back of the room and trailed dolefully out of the basement. He'd never let a mission defeat him before. But this time, with no real leads, he had no idea what to do next. He checked his watch.

4.23 A.M.

Time was running out.

Out in the alley, Zac hopped on his karaoke hover scooter. He was about to roar off when something caught his eye. It was a poster.

GAMES CONVENTION

Bladesville Town Hall

Try out the coolest gaming technology!

OPEN 24 HOURS

Sponsored by MindLab

Zac's spy senses zinged. *If the hackers owned a game console that wasn't even in the shops yet, wasn't it possible they'd be involved in a games convention?*

Zac was going to find out!

He zoomed through the streets of Bladesville towards the town hall. Engaging hover mode, he leapt over rubbish bins and the occasional dog. In less than ten minutes, Zac was there.

Zac stopped the hover scooter near the front entrance and raced inside. Almost immediately, he felt a hand clamp down on his shoulder.

'Excuse me, sir.'

Zac turned and saw a man in a black suit and dark sunglasses smiling grimly.

'Me?' asked Zac, as innocently as he could. He had to pretend to be an ordinary games-mad kid, not the super spy he was.

'Congratulations!' said the man, in a strange voice. 'You've won a wildcard entry into our Grand Games Battle. The best gamers in the world going head-to-head, live on the big screen.'

'Er, no thanks. I'd rather just look around the convention,' said Zac.

There were hundreds of kids milling around. The hackers were in there somewhere, Zac could feel it. He couldn't afford to waste time in some stupid games competition.

'But you've been selected by MindLab, the world's most advanced gaming company. What *normal kid* would pass up a chance like that?' asked the man, his eyes narrowing. 'You are a *normal kid*, right?'

'Oh, totally normal,' said Zac hastily.

'Well, then. Step this way.'

The man slapped a hand on Zac's shoulder and shoved him towards the stage.

Two monitors and two game consoles sat waiting for the players. Overhead, a giant screen had been rigged up so everyone at the convention could see who was playing and how they were scoring.

'You know how to play *Flight Night*, right?' said the man. 'It's a flight-simulator game.' Zac shrugged. He had some experience with flight simulators…

More than most of his opponents, it seemed. One by one, Zac clobbered every challenger. It was easy. *Almost too easy,* thought Zac.

Was someone letting him win?

Pretty soon, Zac found himself in the semi-finals, leading by one point as the

siren sounded. He'd made the grand final!

Zac checked his watch.

Playing in the grand final would take up even more time. But even worse, the 8-year-old kid he'd been playing in the semis burst into tears.

'Hey, don't cry,' said Zac. 'There's always next year.'

The kid nodded, not looking convinced. The poor kid was a total *Flight Night* addict, that was obvious.

Zac gazed up at the big screen above their heads. On the screen, all you could really see of the players was the backs of their heads. The kid's hair was a totally different colour to Zac's, but maybe...

Zac grabbed a bright blue baseball cap from a nearby table of freebies.

'I've got an idea,' he said casually to the kid. 'I'm kind of in a hurry. Could you do me a favour and take my spot in the grand final?'

The kid's eyes lit up.

Zac put the cap on the kid's head. 'Just don't turn around while you're playing,' he said. 'On the screen no-one will know it's not me.

Leaving me free to look for the hackers, Zac added silently to himself.

Zac leapt off the stage. Straight away, the crowd swallowed him up. He was safe, at least for the moment.

He thought over everything Leon told him about the mind-controlled game console the hackers left behind.

It was made by MindLab.

If Zac found the MindLab display here at

the Games Convention, there was a good chance the hackers would be somewhere nearby!

It wasn't hard to spot. Over in the corner, an enormous blinking neon sign read, 'MindLab. Tomorrow's gaming today.'

Zac headed over.

MindLab had set up rows of computers so everyone at the convention could try their games and equipment.

A thrill rushed through Zac. Every kid at every computer at the MindLab display was wearing a high-tech metal helmet! They were testing the MindLab 3000 console. The hackers must be very close now.

But where? Zac needed to hang back

for a while and watch. But it was already 8.01 a.m. Less than an hour until the firewall was breached!

The MindLab display was the most popular stand by far. Kid after kid stepped up to try out the new mind-controlled console. That made sense. *Who wouldn't want to try out something so awesome?*

All the same, Zac couldn't help thinking how rich a company like MindLab must be. *But to keep the money rolling in,* thought Zac, *they need to keep kids addicted to their games.*

Computer games were definitely fun, but there was also something a little bit creepy about the way they sucked you in.

Suddenly, Zac noticed a strange thing.

BOOP!
ZAP!
PEOW!
BEEP!
LEVEL TWO
ZING
HIGH SCORE!
ZAP

When a kid made a very high score, a man in a black suit and dark sunglasses would appear from nowhere. The man would whisper something in the kid's ear and the two of them would disappear through a door. As Zac watched, it happened three times.

Where were the men taking the games champs? And what were they whispering?

Zac dug out his trusty SpyPad. He switched it on and stuck in a pair of head-phones. The SpyPad had a high-powered multi-directional microphone feature. Zac could hear almost anything, even the softest whisper, from about 50 metres away.

Sneaking closer to the MindLab display,

Zac pointed his SpyPad at one of the men in black suits. The man leant down towards one of the kids playing.

'Hey, you're pretty good at that game,' the man said. The kid hardly looked up.

'My name's Mr Tait,' said the man, sticking out his hand. 'How'd you like a job with MindLab? We're hiring champion gamers for an interesting project we're working on. We pay good money.'

That got the kid's attention. He nodded, stood up and walked off with Mr Tait.

Zac followed along behind, as close as he dared. Mr Tait and the kid disappeared through a door that said, 'Private'.

Zac crouched down behind a pot plant

and listened. The SpyPad's microphone was so powerful, Zac could hear everything the man said, even through a closed door.

'MindLab is so much more than a gaming company,' Mr Tait was saying. 'The technology we invent for games, we also use for much bigger things. Like satellites.'

Satellites! Zac's face flushed with excitement. He was about to crack this case, he could feel it.

'At the moment, we're trying to discover how a powerful satellite called WorldEye works,' Mr Tait said. 'Since you're so good with the MindLab 3000, we thought you'd be able to help. We use the same controls for our WorldEye project, you see.'

So the kid on the other side of the door would be joining a group of kids recruited by MindLab to hack into WorldEye using the MindLab 3000. The hackers Zac followed in the karaoke bar were too!

The plan was ingenious. Develop top-level hacking technology and disguise it as an ordinary game console. Then, recruit the best gamers and pay them lots of money for their silence.

No-one would ever suspect kids would be the brains behind a plot as big as hacking into WorldEye.

Just then, the kid on the other side of the door asked Mr Tait a question.

'I thought that satellite belonged to

someone else,' the kid said. Zac held his breath. *What would Mr Tait say to that?*

There was a long silence. Then Zac heard the faintest sound. Even with the powerful SpyPad microphone, it was almost too quiet to hear. It was a cross between a sob and a whimper of pain. Zac's blood ran cold.

Zac heard Mr Tait's cruel voice. 'When you work for MindLab, you don't ever ask questions. Now you know why.'

Pins and needles prickled Zac's legs. He was going to cramp up if he didn't move soon. He shifted a millimetre to his left. But it was enough.

'Over there! Behind the pot plant!'

Oh no! One of the kids from the karaoke bar had spotted Zac.

Before he could run, Zac was surrounded. Zac recognised the man from the front entrance, the one who'd forced him to enter the games comp. He saw all the kids from the karaoke bar. And there were a whole lot of goons he hadn't met yet as well.

There was no escaping this one!

'I know someone very keen to meet you,' said the man from the front entrance in his creepy voice. He grabbed Zac roughly by the arm. 'The head of MindLab, Jimmy Shady.'

Zac looked around for help. Surely there'd be security guards at the Games Convention? Surely they wouldn't just let a whole lot of goons march him away in broad daylight?

But then Zac remembered. MindLab was sponsoring the Games Convention. If there were security guards, they worked for MindLab. They'd be no help at all.

Zac needed a plan. But at the rate the goons were dragging him through the hall, there wasn't much time to come up with one. He'd have to think something up on the spot!

'This way,' said the man from the front entrance, yanking Zac towards a glass office overlooking the entire convention centre.

Magically, the door slid aside. There at a desk was a very short, very ugly man. His thin hair was scraped back against his skull with shiny hair gel. His skin was clammy and pocked like a toad's.

The ugly man stood up and nodded politely. It was like he and Zac were about to sit down to a friendly game of chess.

'Before I kill you,' said the ugly man, 'let me introduce myself.'

Zac knew that a spy must never show fear. Even when his stomach was flip-flopping wildly.

'I'm Jimmy Shady,' said the man. 'Take a seat. I'll tell you all about my operation.'

When he was a kid, Jimmy Shady would've been the last one picked for the footy team. The one who never got invited to anyone's birthday party. The one who ate his lunch all by himself.

Now, Zac could tell Jimmy Shady felt important at last. And he couldn't wait to tell Zac exactly how powerful he really was. In fact, Jimmy Shady was so thrilled with himself, his eyes misted over. He didn't even notice Zac unlocking his SpyPad screen. That suited Zac just fine.

'Being a GIB spy, you've no doubt worked out I'm recruiting games whizzes to help me hack into your precious World-Eye satellite.'

Zac nodded. 'Why would you want to hack into WorldEye? You're head of a games company, not an international spy,' Zac said. The more Jimmy Shady told him, the better.

'Once I control WorldEye, I'll be able to spy on stupid kids like all the ones out there. I'll be able to find out what they like and don't like. That way, I'll get them all hooked on even more of my super-addictive games!'

'How close are you to controlling WorldEye?' asked Zac.

'One line of computer code away.'

Jimmy Shady consulted his notes. 'We know the second-last line is H=//t+13, but we haven't cracked the last line yet. The kids I've recruited today are doing tests right now.'

Zac said nothing.

'Untold riches will be mine! And the funniest part is, I'm using the kids themselves to get even more kids hooked on my games!' Jimmy Shady laughed an evil laugh.

It was all Zac needed to hear. As casually as he could, Zac stretched his arms up. Just the way he'd planned it, something rolled down his sleeve and into his hand.

A stink bomb.

Zac always kept one up his sleeve, just in case. It wasn't anything clever or high-tech. But as Zac was learning, sometimes the old-fashioned gadgets are the best.

With all his might, Zac chucked the stink bomb at the wall.

It exploded.

Instantly the room filled with gas.

Jimmy Shady coughed and spluttered. So did his goons. The gas smelt worse than 10,000 dog farts!

BWA-HA! HA!
?!
?
BOOM!
COUGH
URP
HACK

Zac sprang to his feet. Before anyone knew what was happening, he'd raced out the door.

He'd managed to secretly record Jimmy Shady admitting his evil plan on the mini-video camera in his SpyPad. Zac had all the evidence he needed to arrest Jimmy and stop the hackers cracking the final line of computer code.

But how, in a room crawling with Mind-Lab goons, could one 12-year-old arrest the head of MindLab?

Zac tore through the Games Convention towards the main stage.

With all the monitors and equipment on the stage, the next part of his plan would be easy. As quick as lightning, Zac plugged his SpyPad into the 'Video In' jack on the giant screen.

Zac hit Play. Suddenly, Jimmy Shady's

voice boomed through the Bladesville Town Hall. Everyone stopped what they were doing and looked up. Zac was broadcasting Jimmy Shady's confession for the entire convention to hear.

'Untold riches will be mine! And the funniest part is, I'm using the kids themselves to get even more kids hooked on my games!' Jimmy Shady said.

All across the hall, kids started talking to each other.

'Hear that?'

'The head of MindLab's been messing with gamers!'

'Let's get him! And the hackers!' Zac heard someone yell.

Like a boiling pot about to overflow, the convention erupted. Kids shouted. Game consoles flew through the air.

It was chaos! The gamers stormed Jimmy Shady's glass office. Within moments, he was captured and handcuffed. Soon he was driven away in a police car.

Zac's plan had worked perfectly. His mission was complete – thanks to the kids!

Suddenly, Zac heard his SpyPad bleep.

He'd have to hurry if he was going to make it home in time to put the bins out. But how on earth would he get there? His invisible fighter jet had been stolen by the hackers. There just wasn't time to search for it.

CHINK
POLICE

Zac paced up and down outside Jimmy Shady's office. It was empty now, sealed off with black and yellow crime-scene tape. There was something on the floor, though. Something that looked like. . .yes!

Car keys.

When no-one was looking, Zac grabbed the keys. He wasn't going to *steal* Jimmy Shady's car. More like *borrow* it. Just to drive himself to Bladesville airport so he could get a flight home.

There was always his karaoke hover scooter. But somehow Zac suspected Jimmy Shady would have something much faster, much cooler, he could use.

Zac raced to the car park outside the

Town Hall. There were hundreds of cars parked there!

Which one was Jimmy Shady's?

A remote unlocking device dangled from the key ring. Zac hit the blipper. He heard the sound of a vehicle door unlocking. But Zac couldn't see which car was unlocking its door and flashing its lights.

Zac tried the remote over and over. But not one of the cars seemed to be opening. Zac looked around in frustration.

It was then that he saw it. There was a heli-pad on the roof of the Town Hall. With a brand-new, ultra-light stealth helicopter parked and waiting.

Zac tried the remote once again.

The helicopter's lights came on!

The doors opened!

He'd found his ride home.

As Zac ran towards the heli-pad, a brief doubt flickered through his mind. He'd never actually flown a helicopter before. Then again, in the past 24 hours, he'd piloted a fighter jet, won a gaming comp, hooned around on a hover scooter, sung karaoke and busted Jimmy Shady.

I reckon I can handle a helicopter, thought Zac to himself.

BLOCKBUSTER

CHAPTER 1

It was 4.30 p.m. School was officially over for the day. So why was Zac Power still stuck in a classroom, pretending to look interested in fractions?

Stupid Homework Club, he huffed to himself. Kids whose parents worked late did their homework at Homework Club while they waited to be picked up.

But really, Zac didn't need any teacher watching him while his parents were working. After all, he was a top international spy who'd been on heaps of missions by *himself*.

Zac's brother Leon and their parents were spies, too. They worked for the Government Investigation Bureau, or GIB for short. Zac's parents were taking an advanced code-breaking course. So Zac had to attend Homework Club all week, even though he was 12 years old.

Ms Tran, Zac's teacher, was supervising Homework Club that day. Zac heaved a gusty sigh and flicked open his maths book. Ms Tran looked over at him and smiled.

Isn't learning maths fun? her eyes seemed to twinkle.

Zac tried to keep his eyes open, but it was so hot in the classroom. The air stank of ripe bananas and other people's feet.

Suddenly, there was a knock at the door, and it swung open to a stern figure in a skirt and suit jacket. Mrs De Souza, the school principal!

'Zachary Power,' said Mrs De Souza. 'Please step outside for a moment.'

Zac sat bolt upright. Zachary? This must be serious. Only his parents called him Zachary, and even then, only when he was in big trouble.

The other kids stared as Zac leapt up.

Zac racked his brains for what he could have done. He'd missed a lot of school lately. He'd been so busy on important international missions! But he didn't think he was failing or anything.

'Well, Zac,' said Mrs De Souza, closing the classroom door. 'I don't usually interrupt Homework Club, but the young girl who delivered this insisted that I give it to you straight away.'

Phew! He wasn't in trouble after all – but what was she giving him?

'What was her name again? It started with C…' said the principal, vaguely. 'Never mind,' she finished, handing Zac a glittering gold envelope.

Splashed across the front in curly black letters were the words:

For the urgent attention of
Mr Zachary Power.

His next mission from GIB? It had to be! Although it was weird that everyone was calling him Zachary all of a sudden …

Zac didn't think about it too long. A mission would get him out of Homework Club, and right now that was *all* that mattered.

Zac tore open the envelope. But it wasn't a new mission. It was something even better.

To thank you for so many spying missions accomplished, GIB invites you to the premiere of a blockbuster movie,

COVERT OPERATIONS

Where: Nightshade Theatre, Hollywood.
When: 5 p.m. tomorrow
Dress: Formal
Transportation: Provided

Awesome! Zac was getting out of school, and he didn't even have to stress over any difficult spy work. This time, things would be strictly Mission: Fun.

Zac looked at his watch. He had to get a move on if he wanted to get to Hollywood. The premiere was in 24 hours!

Mrs De Souza asked him how the Homework Club was going, and Zac smiled.

But he wasn't listening. Zac had noticed a strange sound – a kind of low hum unlike anything he'd heard before.

It was a bit like an engine, but it didn't growl like the fighter jet Zac had trained on. It wasn't an ordinary passenger plane either.

'I should probably get going,' Zac said, waggling the gold envelope at Mrs De Souza. She nodded and stalked away.

Zac fished around in his pocket for his SpyPad, the mini-computer that all GIB spies carried.

It had heaps of cool functions, including a powerful mini-telescope. If there was some weird aircraft in the sky, Zac was easily be able to spot it.

Zac raced outside. He looked up, SpyPad at the ready. But Zac didn't need a telescope to see what hovered in the sky above him.

It was an enormous, shiny gold blimp. Across the side, in giant black letters, were the words *Covert Operations*. This bling-covered blimp must be Zac's transportation to Hollywood!

How am I going to get up there, though? he wondered. But before he could blink, a rope swung down from the blimp's cabin.

Zac grabbed the rope. His feet lifted off the ground.

He was headed for Hollywood!

WHOOOOSH!

It seemed slightly weird to Zac that GIB would send a flashy gold blimp to pick him up. Normally GIB was paranoid about being noticed.

But Zac didn't dwell on his doubts for too long. The blimp was even cooler inside than it looked from the outside!

The cabin was carpeted in white fluffy

rugs. Chocolate frogs were heaped into crystal bowls dotted around the cabin.

And although the blimp could have carried lots of people, it looked like Zac was the only passenger.

A woman in a white apron appeared. Zac had never seen her before. *Strange*, he thought. He knew pretty much all the local GIB staff. *Maybe she's from the Hollywood office?*

'Please make yourself comfortable, Mr Power,' she said smoothly.

Zac's reclining seat was soft and wide. He had never travelled in such comfort!

'You can access all the latest movies here,' explained the woman, pointing to a massive plasma screen.

'And this,' she continued, as a machine sprang out of Zac's armrest, 'is your personal popcorn popper.'

The trip was ten hours, which wasn't long enough to enjoy everything on the blimp. First, Zac watched a movie. Then he had a foot massage and head rub. Then he discovered the in-seat virtual-reality roller-coaster rides.

He was still riding *Iron Gutz*, the world's first virtual-reality roller-coaster, when suddenly he felt a bump for real.

Zac checked the time on his SpyPad. It was 3.03 a.m. – nearly time to touch down. Perhaps the bump Zac felt was just the blimp coming in to land?

Then – **EURGH!**

The blimp lurched sideways, leaving Zac's stomach behind. *This is no ordinary landing!* Zac thought, worriedly.

He rushed to the window. Below, the lights of Hollywood lay spread out like Christmas lights. Mansions clung to the steep cliffs, a shimmering aqua swimming pool in every yard.

But none of it explained why the blimp was flying so crazily all of a sudden.

Inside the cabin, crystal bowls smashed on the floor, scattering chocolate frogs everywhere. The lights flickered. *What's going on?* Zac hoped they weren't about to crash.

Zac scanned the skies for an answer. Then he saw it. A chopper was weaving in and out of the blimp's flight path!

What kind of idiot would fly so close to another aircraft? Zac thought furiously. The chopper's blades, whizzing so fast they were a blur, would slice through the blimp's outer lining in a flash!

Zac looked closely at the chopper. Inside the cabin sat a woman with blonde hair piled high on her head. A hairless dog with bulging eyes and a diamond collar lay curled in her lap.

The woman waved her fist in Zac's direction. Zac noticed the sharp red nails, like claws, at the end of her fingers.

C-LURCH!
CRASH!

The woman looked an awful lot like Chrissie L'Estrange, the Hollywood actress. Everybody knew her – it was impossible not to. Chrissie and her little dog Poppet were on the cover of every magazine. Zac hated her movies.

Zac looked again. Now Chrissie was screaming something in his direction!

Zac was glad of his lip-reading training. He could understand her perfectly.

'GET OUTTA MY WAY, JERK!' she screeched. 'DON'T YOU KNOW WHO I AM?' Her chopper swooped in front of the blimp.

Inside the blimp, Zac heard an announcement.

'This is your captain speaking.
We apologise for this unexpected turbulence.
The chopper will land on the helipad
on top of the Hotel Deluxe.
We will land there afterwards.'

Zac thought he heard the captain mutter, 'Even though we were here first.'

A few minutes later, the blimp touched down on the helipad. Chrissie L'Estrange was already there, surrounded by fussing personal assistants.

I'll just go over there and clear things up, thought Zac to himself. But as soon as he took a step in Chrissie's direction, flashbulbs exploded in his eyes.

'Who are you? Are you Chrissie's latest boyfriend?' someone cried out of nowhere. 'What's your name? Who's your agent?'

Zac's mouth fell open. *The paparazzi! Where did they come from?*

'He's no-one,' Zac heard one of them say. 'Let's follow Chrissie.'

And with that, the photographers and reporters scattered from the helipad.

I'm not no-one, Zac wanted to reply. *I'm a top spy here for a big premiere!*

Zac turned back to the blimp. But in the commotion, it had flown off without Zac noticing. Zac's backpack lay on the helipad. All of a sudden, he was alone in Hollywood – the strangest of all strange places.

Zac's ears popped as the super-fast lift swept him up to his penthouse on the 51st floor of the Hotel Deluxe. The doors opened directly into the suite, which was equipped with an ice-cream machine and a wide-screen cinema.

Zac dumped his backpack on the huge king-sized bed.

He clicked on the remote control and a giant TV screen dropped from the ceiling.

An announcer with a stiff wave of blonde hair was beaming at the camera.

'Stay tuned for a Channel One exclusive report into spying in the modern age,' she was saying. 'We reveal how spy agencies are looking for ways to make their investigations quicker and more efficient.'

Leon would probably watch that, the big nerd, thought Zac, smiling to himself.

THUD! THUD! THUD!

Someone was knocking at the door of his suite – loudly!

'Room service!' called a voice.

Zac got up and opened the door.

'Hot dog?' said the pimply guy standing in Zac's doorway. He held out a tray of hot dogs zig-zagged with yellow mustard.

'Er, I didn't order a hot dog,' said Zac.

'Take one, they're delicious!' said the guy, and then he leant in closer.

'I'm a GIB agent,' he muttered. 'We tracked your arrival in the blimp. We've actually been trying to get in touch with you since yesterday, but it seems the lining of the blimp interfered with your SpyPad receptor, and blocked all incoming messages.

'No-one at GIB knows why you're in town,' he added, 'but you've got a new mission. Now take the hot dog.'

He handed Zac a hot dog and left, singing 'have a nice day!' as he went.

Zac stared after him, feeling confused. Why didn't GIB know why Zac was in Hollywood? After all, it was GIB who invited him to the premiere of *Covert Operations*! And if they didn't, who did?

I guess I'd better find out what my mission is, thought Zac as he checked out the hot dog. There was a sticker on the bun, so tiny he had to squint to read it. It said 'FTP enabled'.

The mission must be a file inside the hot dog! But there was a problem. How was Zac going to upload a mission into his SpyPad from a *hot dog*?

?
KNOCK
KNOCK
?

Without smearing mustard on the casing, Zac held the hot dog up to his SpyPad. A green light flickered on. His SpyPad was bluetooth compatible... and so was the hot dog. The mission was uploading wirelessly!

As Zac read the new meassage on the SpyPad, he realised he had two missions. To solve the ThoughtVision mystery and to figure out who'd invited him to the premiere. But the premiere was only 12 hours away!

Before leaving the penthouse suite, Zac paused in front of the mirror to slick some product into his hair. There was no way he wanted to look scruffy on the stylish streets of Hollywood!

CLASSIFIED

MISSION INITIATED 4.54 A.M.

Cinemania, a Hollywood film studio, is spending millions on a mysterious invention called ThoughtVision.

In fact, they're spending more than they do on producing films. This may be innocent, but GIB is suspicious.

YOUR MISSION

Work out what ThoughtVision does and locate a prototype for GIB.

~ END ~

Zac supposed that the obvious place to start the ThoughtVision investigation was at the Cinemania Studios. But before he could hail a taxi, a vehicle pulled up right in front of him.

The passenger door opened and a voice wafted out. 'Please, come inside.'

Zac had to step back to take in the full size of the car. It was a yellow stretch Hummer. Its engine rumbled loudly.

Zac climbed in. But there was no-one driving the car! The voice, which was obviously computerised, said, 'Welcome to AutoJeeves, the driverless chauffeur service. Where would you like to go?'

'Cinemania Studios,' replied Zac.

Ah, the Hollywood lifestyle, thought Zac, as the stretch Hummer took off.

The Hummer pulled up outside the fancy iron gates of Cinemania. Through the fence, Zac could see row after row of sets from old movies. There were people everywhere, zipping around the huge studio lot in white golf carts, or sitting around in canvas chairs with their names on the back. The studio must keep shooting movies all night!

A security guard stood at the gates, where a queue of people waited to get in.

'Yes? What business do you have here?' asked the guard mechanically.

'I have a script meeting with Mr Spielford,' Zac heard someone say.

'I am Chrissie L'Estrange's new plastic surgeon,' said a woman just in front of Zac.

'You?' the guard asked Zac.

A big part of spying was pretending to be someone you weren't. But Zac was totally exhausted. It had been a long night. For once, he struggled to think of a false identity. 'I've got an appointment with Poppet L'Estrange,' blurted Zac at last. 'I'm ... I'm ... I'm her hair stylist.'

The guard eye-balled Zac silently.

I'm such an idiot! Zac panicked. *Who'd believe a hairless dog has its own hairdresser?*

Zac's spirits plummeted. No way would he get past the security guard and into Cinemania now!

Was the unthinkable about to happen? Was Zac Power actually going to fail a mission?

'Poppet L'Estrange?' repeated the guard.

'Er, yes,' said Zac, uncertainly.

'What time is your appointment?'

Zac checked his watch. It was 5.37 a.m.

'Six o'clock,' Zac said, sounding more confident than he felt.

'It's that trailer over there,' said the guard finally, opening the gates.

The guard shook his head in pity. 'You're Poppet's fourth stylist this month.'

I guess nothing's too weird for Hollywood, Zac thought.

Zac headed in the direction of Poppet L'Estrange's trailer to avoid suspicion. All the stars (and their dogs) had their own luxury trailers to sit in between filming scenes. The more famous the star, the bigger the trailer.

That must be someone really important, Zac thought as he passed a silver trailer the size of a road train, complete with a satellite dish on top. There was a name on the door in a star-shaped tag that said 'Caroline'.

I wonder who that is? thought Zac.

Then Zac noticed a golf cart puttering to a stop nearby. A woman got out, yakking into her mobile phone.

'We aim to supply each unit with a camera by next year,' she said. 'It will cost a lot at first, but think of the savings later on.'

The woman was so wrapped up in her conversation, she left the keys in the golf cart's ignition as she walked off.

Seizing his chance, Zac jumped into the golf cart and sped off. Now he could search Cinemania properly!

Zac was flying over a speed bump when the golf cart's radio crackled to life.

'Attention all security units. A golf cart has been stolen. Suspect has cool hair, repeat cool hair. Likely identity: Zachary Power.'

Ah-ha! Cinemania was definitely not a genuine movie studio! Otherwise, how would they know his name?

Suddenly, Zac heard a weird crunching sound behind him. There, not ten metres away, was a security guard in a golf cart, cracking his knuckles!

The guard's neck was as thick as a power pole. He looked more machine than human. And he was heading in Zac's direction – FAST!

Zac slammed his foot on the accelerator. His cart shot forward, but not fast enough. The guard was closing in! Zac sped towards what looked like the Wild Wild West.

It was actually an old film set, cluttered with horse troughs and abandoned mine shafts.

Desperately, he wove between the obstacles. This was harder than *Mario Kart*! And if he crashed, Zac knew he couldn't just start all over again.

Zac slammed into a barrel and sent it flying. The cart flipped. Zac flew out and …

KER-RUNCH!

He landed flat on his face. The barrel slammed into the guard's cart, knocking him over like a skittle.

Zac jumped up and ran for it.

Gotta hide, he thought. His face stung from where he'd landed on the gravel.

Up ahead, Zac saw a haunted house set from a horror movie. The windows were boarded up, the door nailed shut.

Perfect ... if I can figure out how to get in.

Frantically, Zac rattled every board on every window.

RIIIIP!

A board came loose and Zac wriggled through the window. Velvety darkness swallowed him up instantly.

Blindly, he felt his way further inside the house. All of a sudden, Zac went cold. *What was that sound?*

Footsteps!

'Zac Power!' thundered a voice.

The room flooded with yellow light.

Zac's eyes throbbed. He'd been caught!

Standing in front of him was the guard from before! Hang on, hadn't Zac left him behind outside?

Wait ... thought Zac. *What's that weird lump on his neck?*

An ON button! No wonder this guard looked like the one from the cart.

And like the one at the front gate, Zac realised.

The guards were all androids!

A new GIB ruling required all spies to wear PitStink capsules under their arms in case of android attack. When broken, the capsule releases a vile stink from the armpit.

STOMP! STOMP!
FLAP! FLAP! FLAP! FRRRT
FSSSHHH!
POP!
ZZZT! BZZ

As hard as he could, Zac pumped his right arm up and down three times until he felt a blast of gas.

'Halt, Zac Power,' boomed the android.

Zac lifted his right arm. Powerful stink waves wafted out – a cross between rotting meat and dog farts.

'Halt, Zac Pow– errrrgh!' screeched the android. It dropped to the floor, holding its nose. Smoke curled from its ears. The PitStink had short-circuited its wiring!

Hastily, Zac stepped over the android. He had a sense that somewhere in this building there was a clue about ThoughtVision. *Why else would it be guarded so closely?* Zac thought. *And by fierce, ruthless androids?*

In one corner, Zac spotted an old staircase.

Could lead to an attic, Zac thought, placing a sneaker on the first step. *That's the perfect place to hide information about ThoughtVision.*

Suddenly –

Fffffffftftftftftftftft!

A flock of bats appeared from nowhere and flew straight at Zac's face!

Zac's heart pounded, but he pushed the bats aside and reminded himself that he was in a haunted house. The bats were on strings. They were made of rubber!

Just part of the film set, Zac reminded himself, breathing quickly.

He kept climbing the stairs. At the top was a very small door. Zac firmly pushed it open.

What lay behind was no dusty old attic! Instead, there were rows and rows of high-tech laptops. Zac's spy senses tingled. He was onto something!

Zac raced to the nearest computer and selected Display Recent Documents. There it was – ThoughtVision_Blueprints.doc!

Zac clicked. The screen filled with diagrams. On the left, Zac saw a picture of a movie camera. A bunch of wavy lines labelled ThoughtWaves wiggled towards it. Labels and arrows pointed in all directions.

Zac's brain hurt trying to understand it all. He needed Leon's help. He plugged his SpyPad into the laptop, uploaded the diagrams then punched in Leon's number.

He glanced at his watch.

7.47 A.M.

Leon would be up by now. But when Zac tried to call, there was no signal!

Gotta get outside, Zac thought. He ran in the direction of the stairs, but then changed his mind.

The android might have rebooted his system by now, he thought.

During his GIB Spy Academy training, Zac had learnt heaps of tricky escapes. Now was the time to try one out!

Zac jumped onto a chair and punched out a skylight overhead. He was going to attempt a Multi-Storey Roof Jump, an escape reserved for the bravest of spies.

Zac wriggled through the skylight and onto the roof. As he looked over the edge, he heard a noise on the staircase inside. The android was back! *Good thing I didn't take the stairs*, Zac thought.

If he took a big run-up and timed it perfectly ... yes, he probably could jump off the building and land on the roof of the moving golf cart below. No android guard would think of looking for him there!

The golf cart was in the perfect position. It was now or never!

He sped towards the edge of the building. He took a deep breath and … JUMPED!

He was in free fall … and then … **THUNK!**

Zac landed squarely on the cart's roof.

'What was that?' came a girl's voice from inside the cart.

Zac froze. He *knew* that voice …

An image flashed into his mind of the enormous silver trailer that he'd seen earlier.

BUMP
VROOM!
VROOOOOM!

He remembered the name 'Caroline' written on the door ...

Caz is short for Caroline! Zac realised with a shock.

Caz was an enemy spy for the enemy organisation BIG. And if Caz was here at Cinemania, that meant the two were somehow linked. *But how?*

Zac was racking his brains when he felt a text message come through on his SpyPad.

Lucky he'd set it to Vibrate mode!

Have you heard the news? BIG's profits 50% down. Ha Ha Ha. – Leon.

Now wasn't the time for spy industry gossip! Zac needed proper help from Leon, like an online search to work out how BIG and Cinemania were related.

But I can't call Leon from here! Caz will hear every word! thought Zac.

There was only one thing to do.

He flung himself sideways, rolling off the cart and landing heavily in the gutter with a muffled 'urgh!'

Just as he had planned, the cart kept on driving. He didn't think anyone had seen him jump off.

Right, now to call Leon, Zac thought, dusting off his T-shirt and digging out his SpyPad.

Then he heard a booming voice. 'There you are!'

Oh no, the android guards! Zac panicked.

'You're needed on set, Grave,' continued

the voice, which belonged to a beefy man wearing a 'Film Crew' T-shirt. His name was stitched on the back – Brutus.

Brutus grabbed Zac's arm. There was no getting away. Brutus gripped like an angry pit-bull.

'You're ready for your big stunt scene, right?' said Brutus.

Stunt scene? Zac's brain whirred.

There was a child star called Dave 'Grave' Danger – the most extreme stuntman ever. He was 12, Zac's age. Brutus must have seen Zac's commando roll and mistaken him for Grave!

'In here,' said Brutus, steering Zac into a film studio as big as an aircraft hanger.

On the door, a sign read:

Action/blockbuster: Short Fuse
CAUTION
Filming in progress

Zac looked around. The studio was crawling with people wheeling cameras and shouting into megaphones. Straight away, someone rushed towards Zac and fluffed his hair. His nose was dabbed with make-up.

The make-up part was weird. Zac had hated it when enemy agents had given him a make-over as revenge, and he sure didn't like it now!

Still, he thought, *it's nice to be treated like a star for once.*

'OK, Grave,' said Brutus, checking a clipboard. 'First up is the scene where you run through a glass window.'

Zac nodded. *No worries! Bet they pre-shatter the glass so it only* looks *like you're breaking it*, he thought.

'Then,' said Brutus, 'you wrestle Bessie.'

The entire set went silent as Brutus led Bessie in on a massive silver chain. Bessie was a wild black bear!

In a lame attempt to make her look friendly, someone had tied a pink collar around Bessie's neck. It didn't work. Bessie's lips were peeled back in a snarl, giving Zac a perfect view of her big, white fangs dripping with gloopy spit. Great.

BRUSH! BRUSH!
VOOOOM!
CREW
BRUTUS
GRAR!

Spy school didn't cover wrestling black bears. *But if Dave 'Grave' Danger can do it, so can I*, figured Zac.

He quickly glanced at his watch, and grimaced. It was already 8.31 a.m.!

Zac desperately needed to keep going with the mission. But if he told the crew he wasn't Dave 'Grave' Danger, they'd call security. And Zac didn't want to mess with those androids again.

Then he had an idea. He let out a high-pitched scream.

'Where is the lemon-flavoured orange drink and brownies I asked for? I cannot work under these conditions!' He tossed his head and pouted. 'I WANT to go back to my dressing room RIGHT NOW.'

Zac was stacking on his best impression of a celebrity tantrum.

And when I'm back in Grave's dressing room, I'll sneak off, Zac thought.

The crew just stood and watched Zac's tantrum. No-one seemed surprised.

'OK, Grave,' said Brutus. 'I get it. You're too scared to wrestle Bessie.'

Too scared? *I'm not too scared*, Zac huffed to himself. *I'm just too busy!* But he couldn't go back to the dressing room now. The next quickest way out was for him to just wrestle Bessie and then make a run for it afterwards.

'Forget the brownies,' said Zac sulkily.

Brutus lead Zac over to a thick piece of glass. On the other side, he could just make out the blurry shape of Bessie standing on her hind legs, flexing her claws.

'Quiet, please,' called a voice. 'Roll camera – and – ACTION!'

CRACK!

Zac smashed into the glass window at top speed. Glass showered down around him.

Cool! he thought. *Now to wrestle Bess–*

WHUMP!

Bessie landed heavily on Zac's back, growling dangerously.

It was like being hugged by a loving aunt – who's hairy and stinks of salmon.

Suddenly Zac remembered something

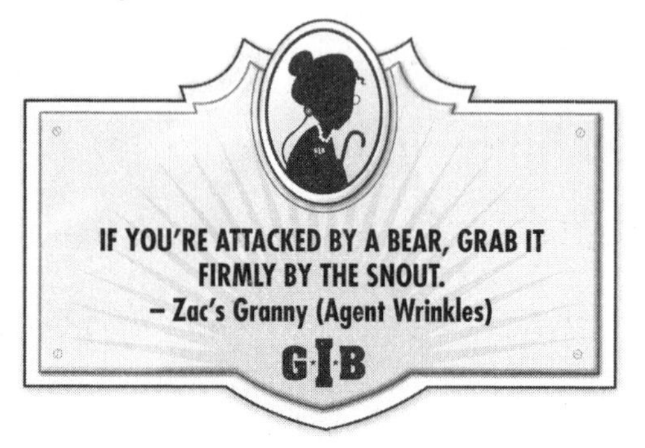

his grandma had told him.

Or was that alligators? wondered Zac. His grandma tended to talk a lot. Either way, now was the time to try out her advice!

Zac grabbed Bessie's slobbery muzzle. The enormous bear gave a 'humph?' of surprise. Then she let go of Zac! She rubbed her snout and looked hurt.

'CUT!' yelled the director. 'Not bad, Grave. But you need to look … braver. Let's do it again.'

Zac shrugged. Surely it wouldn't be long until he could sneak away …

'ACTION!' bellowed the director.

Zac ran towards a second sheet of glass. But before he got there, the director yelled out, 'CUT!'

What now? thought Zac, frustrated.

'There's a hair on the camera lens. Let's go again.'

Now Zac could understand why it sometimes took a whole year to make a movie! After every take, a new sheet of glass had to be brought in.

Bessie's fur was brushed and Zac's make-up touched up.

Precious time slipped away. 9.12 a.m. 10.43 a.m. Soon it was midday!

'OK, let's break for lunch,' called the director at last.

'I'll be in my trailer!' Zac answered, disappearing into the shadows.

The back of the studio was a jumble of camera equipment, lights and dusty old sets.

Anything could be hidden back here, thought Zac. *Hey – what's that?*

Zac noticed a door, bolted shut. A sign read, 'Camera Tests'.

Something clicked in Zac's mind. Those blueprints said ThoughtVision was some kind of camera.

This might get the mission back on track, thought Zac.

Zac grabbed the SpyPad from his pocket and flipped it over. He slid the back casing off and pulled out a skeleton key. It was a special GIB issue key that could open any lock in the world.

Zac jiggled the key in the lock. It was stiff, but it opened. He inched the huge metal door open. Pressing close to the walls, he sneaked into the room.

A man sat on a chair facing away from Zac. He was looking into a movie camera.

Zac couldn't quite make out who was behind the camera.

'You can trust me,' the man sitting in the chair said. He sounded like he was about to cry.

Then Zac noticed a screen above the man's head. As soon as the man said anything, the screen displayed different words above his head.

'I would never betray BIG,' the man stammered. But the screen said:

I HATE BIG.

'I know what you're *really* thinking!' said a girl from behind the camera.

It sounded like Caz. And she was obviously using a ThoughtVision camera.

What evil technology! A camera that read thoughts as it filmed. But why would BIG want a camera like that?

Suddenly, the pieces dropped into place in Zac's mind. BIG's profits were down. And that news report, back in the hotel, had said spies needed quicker ways to work!

Questioning people with a camera that read minds would be *the* quickest possible way to find out all sorts of secrets. It would be way more reliable than any truth serum or special investigations.

A movie studio would be the perfect front for an operation like ThoughtVision. BIG probably invented Cinemania to cover its tracks.

That explained why the films Cinemania made were so terrible. A movie like *Short Fuse*, where a kid wrestled a bear, would be box office poison!

'Soon we'll have people working these cameras full-time,' Caz crowed. 'We can't afford to waste our own good people on boring work like that.'

'I see,' said the man in the chair. But the screen displayed his true thoughts:

I HATE YOU!

'We're going to brainwash enemy spies, including that loser Zac Power,' said Caz, starting to giggle. 'Zac Power's going to work for BIG!'

At that moment, all Zac wanted in the world was to yank Caz's bushy pigtail.

How would BIG try to brainwash him? And more importantly, how dare Caz call him a loser?

He was furious, but he took some deep breaths. Stay calm, he told himself, *she's about to spill the beans on her evil plan*.

'Using Cinemania Studios as our front, we've shot a new spy movie, *Covert Operations*,' said Caz, sounding thrilled with herself. 'It's packed with subliminal messages.'

Subliminal messages? thought Zac. He knew they were words or pictures in a film that flashed up too fast for you to notice. Subliminal messages could convince you to do things against your will. *Things like working for BIG!*

Suddenly, he heard something. *Beep! Beep!* It was getting louder.

Annoyed, Caz looked up from the ThoughtVision camera. 'What is it, G5-382?' she snapped.

There was the clank of metal. Zac peered out from behind a stack of boxes.

Another android security guard!

'Heat sensors engaged,' said the android in its dull robotic voice.

'What?' asked Caz, irritably.

'Human heat detected in north-east quadrant of the room,' droned the android.

Oh no! Zac was busted!

The ThoughtVision camera was so close and bringing back that prototype was an essential part of his mission! But if Zac didn't scram right that very second, Caz and BIG would get him for sure.

I'll have to capture the camera some other way, Zac thought grimly.

He scanned the room for ways to escape. But Caz had blocked one door, and the android was guarding the other!

There was an air vent high up on the wall. Zac lunged onto a wobbly stack of packing crates. He leapt at a pipe running along the ceiling. Then, swinging like a monkey along the pipe, he kicked in the air vent.

Now to wriggle through the hole …

'It's Zac Power!' Caz squealed. 'You androids are supposed to be saving us money. Now show me you're worth it! Get him!'

It was a squeeze, but luckily Zac was just small enough to slip through the vent.

There was no way the massive metal android could follow him!

Zac popped out the other side, Caz's furious screams ringing in his ears.

Zac spotted a brand-new black Harley Davidson parked nearby. He grabbed his GIB skeleton key and started the ignition. The Harley rumbled to life.

Zac's SpyPad bleeped an alarm.

1.33 P.M.

Zac still had just enough time to stop the premiere, and capture the ThoughtVision camera.

Zac realised Caz would be at the premiere, and she could lead him to the prototype.

Zac tapped 'Nightshade Theatre' into his SpyPad's GPS system, and roared out of the studio lot.

His mind was racing as fast as the bike. There'd probably be a red carpet at the premiere, and paparazzi taking photos.

Zac checked his outfit. Skate shoes, sweaty T-shirt, dirty jeans. His hair product had long since melted away.

He couldn't turn up to a red carpet event looking like that. A spy has standards!

Zac needed a cool new suit. Not too formal, maybe a scruffy jacket and skinny trousers, like rock stars wear.

But where would I get something like that? Zac wondered.

'Turn left here for the Hollywood Walk of Fame,' said the SpyPad in his pocket. 'Shopping mall and the Nightshade Theatre.'

Just what Zac needed!

With a screech of tyres, Zac took a sharp left onto the Hollywood Walk of Fame. He pulled up outside a shop called Leroy's Outfitters to the Stars.

The shop was packed with amazing clothes. One wall was full of T-shirts, another of motorbike boots. He'd never seen so much cool stuff in one place before. He just couldn't leave without trying a few things on. Surely he had time …

A few outfits later, the sound of the radio snapped him back to reality.

'Another sunny day in Hollywood. The time is 3.00 p.m.'

Zac raced out of the shop with his new

suit on. He'd wasted too much time! He had to get to the Nightshade Theatre.

Zac was concentrating so hard, he didn't notice a shadowy figure behind him –

Ugh!

Someone shoved him in the back!

Zac tumbled forward, his hands out in front of him to break his fall.

But it wasn't hard concrete he felt as he fell. It was something squishy.

WET CEMENT!

Zac was on the Hollywood Walk of Fame, where stars left their handprints in the cement. And someone had replaced the ordinary footpath with the quick-drying kind. Zac was stuck fast!

He looked around for help, but everyone was busily rushing into shops. Joggers wearing sweatbands jumped over him and glamorous mothers pushing prams swerved around him.

Time raced on. 3.17 p.m. 4.06 p.m. 4.45 p.m.! But Zac wasn't going anywhere.

Until he remembered something.

Leon made him keep a DynaWrite pen in his pocket at all times. 'You might need it to do Sudoku puzzles,' he'd said. 'The explosive device hidden inside could be useful, too.'

If Zac could detonate the DynaWrite pen, he could explode the cement around his hands and escape.

But how am I going to get the pen out of my pocket when my hands are stuck fast? Zac wondered.

Zac was no gymnast, but his spy training kept him strong and flexible. If he could get upside down, the DynaWrite pen might drop out of his pocket.

He launched himself skywards. Kicking his legs wildly, he held the handstand. But the explosive pen stayed in his pocket!

Zac wiggled his body. He felt the pen moving. He wiggled a bit more.

At last! The DynaWrite pen fell out onto the cement.

Now, to detonate! thought Zac, kicking his legs down.

?!
SPLAT!
CLICK!
BOOM!

He didn't know the rules on detonating an explosive device with your nose. Perhaps there weren't any?

Hardly daring to breathe, Zac tapped the red button on the end of the pen with the tip of his nose. He leant back as –

BOOOOM!

His hands were free! And his nose was still attached to his face!

He checked the time on his watch.

Zac was too late. *Covert Operations* had already begun!

The movie had started, but Zac wasn't quitting. Showering concrete dust, he ran down the Hollywood Walk of Fame towards the Nightshade Theatre.

Zac knew he had to get inside the cinema to stop innocent spies being brainwashed. But if he saw a single second of the film, he could be brainwashed himself!

I need protection, he thought. He pulled on his sunglasses. Then he stuffed his iPod earphones in, turning the music up loud. *BIG could have planted subliminal messages in the soundtrack, too*, he figured.

Zac ran up the red carpet. Paparazzi were everywhere.

'Look!' someone yelled. 'It's Poppet L'Estrange's stylist!'

'Great suit!' called a TV interviewer, as Zac raced past and into the theatre.

His throat was dry. Passing the candy bar, he grabbed a bucket-sized soft drink.

Zac burst into the cinema where the film was screening. The audience was packed with spies. Some he recognised from GIB!

He avoided looking at the screen. Zac scanned the walls for the projector. He had to stop the screening!

But how? In his mind Zac ran through his gadgets.

Electronic snake-charmer? No good.

Edible dictionary? No way.

How about my trusty slingshot?

Zac felt in his pockets for ammo, but they were empty. Everything must have fallen out when he did the handstand back on the Hollywood Walk of Fame.

What else in a cinema was small and round? ChocBalls!

That'll do! thought Zac, snatching a box from a dazed spy sitting nearby.

Zac whipped round to the back of the cinema. High up on the wall was the projector, safe behind thick glass. *But the ChocBalls feel too light!* If he wanted to smash the projector, Zac calculated that he'd have to hit it in exactly the same place ten times in a row. That would take superior shooting!

He loaded his slingshot with the first ChocBall, and snapped the rubber band.

It whizzed through the air – and hit the glass dead centre. Zac reloaded with a second ChocBall.

THUNK!

The second ChocBall made contact.

'What's that noise?' asked an usher.

He looked familiar to Zac …

The usher was another android! In fact, Zac suddenly realised, all the ushers in the cinema were androids.

Desperately, Zac fired more ChocBalls at the projector.

Seven – eight – nine –

Android ushers appeared from every direction. They were closing in on Zac.

Zac loaded his tenth ChocBall. He took aim, screwing one eye shut for a better view.

But as Zac prepared to fire, an android usher ran up behind him. Its robotic arm reached out towards Zac's neck just as he fired the tenth ball.

SNAP!

It shattered the glass and the projector behind it in a shower of sparks. The cinema screen blanked out.

The audience erupted. Spies jumped out of their seats. Android ushers tried to stop anyone leaving. A girl who sounded very much like Caz screamed, 'Nooooooo!'

Zac spun round. An android was almost on top of him! Lightning fast, Zac tipped the entire bucket-sized soft drink over its head.

Instantly, the acids and sugars in the drink ate through the android's synthetic skin. The android dropped to the floor, one eyeball hanging out on a single piece of red wire.

I really should stay away from soft drinks, thought Zac, as the android shuddered and sparked.

Then a blurry figure raced past Zac. Bushy pigtail, a camera bag over her shoulder – Caz! *And she's probably carrying the ThoughtVision prototype!*

Zac took off after Caz and the prototype. But Caz, sneaky as ever, handed the camera bag to an android usher and ran off.

Should I capture Caz, or stay and secure the prototype? Zac wondered. He hated Caz more than Homework Club. But his mission was to secure the prototype!

He sighed. Caz streaked away as Zac turned to the android.

'You know, I've heard there's a top agent here looking for androids to star in a new movie,' said Zac slyly.

'Really?' said the android, loosening its grip on the camera bag. 'Where?'

'Oh, somewhere over there,' said Zac vaguely, pointing across to the other side of the cinema.

The android spun around for a better look. Zac slipped the camera bag from its arm and ran.

The Harley was still parked where Zac had left it, outside the cinema. He roared off, slinging the camera bag over his shoulder. He called Leon and put him on speaker.

'Leon! Can you get me out of here?' he yelled over the Harley's growl. 'I've got the prototype!'

'I'll plot your co-ordinates on GIB's central mission computer,' said Leon.

Zac heard a crash as a bunch of android ushers burst out of the Nightshade Theatre and started chasing him down the street.

'Will it take long?' yelled Zac.

'Nope,' Leon said. 'There's a GIB rescue chopper in your area. Ride to the Hollywood sign on top of the hill, climb up and we'll grab you from there.'

'Got it,' said Zac, speeding off.

The Hollywood sign loomed in front of him.

THE NIGHTSHADE THEATRE
SCREEE...

He leapt off the Harley and raced to the bottom of the enormous letter 'H'. It was a least ten stories high and made of flat steel.

It would be really difficult to climb. Difficult that is, if Zac's shoes hadn't been specially modified for situations like this.

He flipped the Octopod Mode switch on the tongue of his left shoe. At once, powerful suckers sprung out of the soles. Zac stepped onto the letter 'H' and started walking up.

He was almost at the top when he heard voices below – he was being followed!

'Hey, Grave! You're needed for another stunt!' called Brutus.

'You told me there was an agent looking for androids!' snarled the android usher.

'What's your plan for Poppet L'Estrange's next look?' called a reporter.

But the whirring chopper blades drowned them out. The chopper door opened and the GIB rescue team threw a rope down to Zac. He grabbed hold of it and was instantly hauled upwards to safety.

As soon as he sat down inside the chopper, Zac's SpyPad rang. It was a call from Agent Bum Smack – Zac's mum.

'I hear GIB invited you to a premiere,' said his mum. 'Lucky thing! You'd better write a thank you note to GIB as soon as you get home.'

'Sure, Mum,' said Zac. He could fill her in on what really happened later on.

'Did you enjoy the movie?' his mum asked.

'Yeah, I really got into it,' said Zac, laughing. 'Especially the stunt scenes.'

ZAC POWER

MISSION CHECKLIST!

How many have YOU read?